DOGS

D O G S
ALL ABOUT THEM

by Alvin and Virginia Silverstein

With an Introduction by John C. McLoughlin

illustrated with photographs

Lothrop, Lee & Shepard Books   New York

Library of Congress Cataloging in Publication Data
Silverstein, Alvin. Dogs, all about them.
Bibliography: p. Includes index. Summary: Discusses the evolution of dogs and their uses throughout history and includes information on different breeds, training, care as pets, relationship with
people, and relevant topics.
1.   Dogs—Juvenile   literature.   [1.   Dogs]   I.   Silverstein,   Virginia   B.   II.   Title
SF426.5.S54   1985   636.7   84-29723

ISBN 0-688-04805-6

For Melissa Woodruff

ACKNOWLEDGMENTS

The authors would like to thank John C. McLoughlin for his patient and painstaking reading of the manuscript and helpful comments. Warm thanks are also due to Dr. Linda Cork of Johns Hopkins University, Lorna Coppinger of the New England Farm Center, and Steve Moore of the XVIII Airborne Corps for their invaluable consultation and help. Thanks, too, to all those who kindly supplied photographs for the book, and, last, to Laura and Kevin for their conscientious and loving care of Jacqui.

5

Table of Contents

Courtesy Alvin and Virginia Silverstein.
"Heel!" Dogs are normally trained to walk on their owner's left side.

Introduction

Few symbioses between different animal species are as intimate, complex, and mutually reinforcing as that between human beings and dogs. Enduring across tens of thousands of years, this relationship ranges in character from parasitic to mutualistic, from repellently cruel to staunchly loving. Shifting in character from place to place and time to time, it finds perhaps its most widespread expression in the communion between people and the dogs they keep as pets, the truest of friends.

In *Dogs: All About Them*, Alvin and Virginia Silverstein examine all facets of this endlessly variable link between *Homo sapiens* and *Canis familiaris*. The book is aptly titled, for here we find far more than a treatise on dogs as pets, a listing of breeds, or a training manual: the authors examine the dog as a biological phenomenon whose structure, genetics, ancestry, evolution, senses, and behavior all contribute to its special place in our lives.

Beginning with an informative nontechnical examination of the evolution of the broader canine family, the Silversteins recount our best current understanding of the early process of domestication by which wolves joined our own ancestors in the hunt for food—a way of life to which both species were differently yet superbly adapted. Continuing with a highly readable in-depth look at the characteristics common to all domestic dogs, they detail ways in which the bones, physiology, and behavior of these animals have been manipulated by centuries of breeding to produce from wolflike ancestors the hundreds of breeds we see today. Sensory capabilities, expressive patterns, social, territorial, and mating behaviors, the birth, growth, and even dreaming of dogs are discussed, serving to introduce C. *familiaris* as a complex and intelligent being in its own right. In a nation where dogs are too often regarded as mere furry toys, this approach is indeed refreshing.

Only after this background is established do the Silversteins make an accounting of dog breeds, adhering for the most part to the American Kennel Club's current list of 127 divided into seven functional groups. A brief description of the history, character, and form of most breeds provides an invaluable aid to those readers considering the purchase of a purebred dog. Most commendably, the authors conclude this section with a good hard cautionary look at distorted breeding practices and their resultant injury to so many otherwise noble strains of dogs.

In the United States, of course, most dogs of whatever sort are kept as pets, as friends and companions. Hence the Silversteins take special care in discussing this close physical and emotional relationship between two such complicated (and often unpredictable) animals as dogs and people. Selection, training, health, feeding, showing, and breeding of dogs—and canine birth control—are treated in a manner that simultaneously demystifies and ensures respect for the many responsibilities incurred by dog owners.

Wolves probably originally entered the human bailiwick as hunting partners, coworkers in the never-ending ancestral task of finding meat. Their domesticated descendants continue to excel as workers, and the Silversteins portray the many modern jobs uniquely suited to dogs. As shepherds, lifeguards, police assistants, and soldiers, they perform many tasks to which their senses, speed, and strength bring a new dimension of efficiency. As specialized Seeing-Eye and Hearing Ear companions, dogs offer safety and independence to thousands of people who in former times would have led somberly restricted lives; as alert and empathetic pets they lengthen the life spans of the elderly, the shut-in, and the chronically ill. Dogs even become actors, and the authors share with us the life stories of several famous dogs of television and cinema.

Not all of the dog-human symbiosis is so mutually beneficial; often it becomes quite sadly one-sided. The Silversteins do not balk at discussing the darker aspect of our relationship with dogs, noting that more than thirteen million unwanted dogs and cats are killed each year in American animal shelters. Too, they recount the many dangers of the disgusting practice of abandoning dogs: not only are ownerless dogs' lives "nasty, brutish, and short," but these miserable beasts can become destructive and even deadly in their sorry efforts to feed themselves without the aid of conscientious owners.

And there is always "sport," with its all too frequent overtones of barbarism-for-enjoyment. Dogs are made to fight one another, often to the death, entire breeds of canine gladiators having been devised to sate the ancient human bloodlust. For centuries dogs have also been employed in the killing of tethered bears, bulls, swine, and other animals for the amusement of paying human onlookers, and even carefully regulated modern dog racing knows frequent episodes of cruelty. In connection with these pitiful situations, the Silversteins examine in detail the place of dogs in medical and other scientific experimentation. Here, in a laudably open-minded discussion of the part played by dogs in the advancement of surgical techniques, disease control, and the exploration of space, we find an honesty and objectivity all too rarely encountered in writings on this difficult subject.

The Silversteins conclude with a look at the wild canid species—foxes, jackals, wild dogs, coyotes, and wolves—and their various econiches and behaviors. Ending in this manner, the book reminds us yet again of the complexity and sagacity of the canine kind, and hence of our own pet dogs—a dip into natural history amply reinforcing the respect and care for dogs emphasized by the authors throughout.

Dog owners themselves, Dr. and Mrs. Silverstein share some of their personal experiences, introducing us to dogs they have known and offering not only an extensive bibliography but also a sampling of intriguing quotations about dogs from throughout history and around the world. With its wealth of information and endearingly forthright, balanced tone, *Dogs: All About Them* will be a welcome addition to the libraries not only of dog owners but of readers of any age with an interest in the whys and wherefores of animal life.

JOHN C. MCLOUGHLIN,
author of *The Canine Clan*
and *The Tree of Animal Life*
Tesuque, New Mexico

Courtesy Mary Bloom

A Man's Best Friend

A distant fire alarm woke us in the early morning hours one day last year. We wondered uneasily where the fire might be. Later we found out, when we went down to the center of town to pick up the morning papers. There had been no newspapers delivered to the general store that day. Main Street was blocked by fire trucks, and the store was a smoldering ruin. Within minutes the fire had swept through the old wooden building. But no one was hurt, even though the owners and their three small children were sleeping in the apartment over the store when the fire broke out. Blackie, the family's pet Labrador, barked an alarm in the backyard at the first signs of smoke. The dog's barking woke the family just in time: flames were already shooting up through the floorboards as they escaped from the house.

Dogs have been living with people for a long time—perhaps as long as twenty thousand years. For

This bronze statuette of a man with his hunting dog dates from ca. 1500 B.C. and reflects the already firmly established bond between humans and dogs.

Stone Age humans, dogs were valuable hunting partners, and they guarded the family at home, too. Later, as sheep, goats, and cattle were domesticated, dogs helped in herding and guarding their masters' animals. Today few of us earn our livings by hunting or herding, but dogs have still kept a firm place in our hearts and homes. There are nearly fifty million pet dogs in the United States alone, more than any other kind of pet.

Why have dogs remained so popular? It is useful to have a combination fire and burglar alarm around the house, but the dog's role as a protector is only a small part of the answer. No other animal provides its owners with as much loyalty and devotion as a dog.

WHAT IS A DOG?

Looking at a picture of a Chihuahua, a small child will point without hesitation and say, "Dog." A picture of a Saint Bernard will bring just as prompt a response. "Dog!" the child declares. And yet the tiny, delicate Chihuahua, with its upstanding ears and pointed muzzle, seems to have very little in common with the huge, bulky Saint Bernard; and neither of them looks very much like a wolf or a fox, which a young child might also call a "dog."

Just what do Chihuahuas and Saint Bernards, collies and dachshunds, spaniels, terriers, bulldogs, German Shepherds, and all the other breeds of domestic dogs have in common? And how do they differ from their wild relatives, such as wolves, foxes, and jackals?

All of the dogs, both the wild ones and the domestic dogs, are mammals: warm-blooded animals that are covered with a coat of fur and feed their young with milk produced in the mother's body. Humans are mammals, too (although our fur coat is hardly the

equal of a dog's), and so are many of the other familiar animals, from tiny mice to huge elephants, from
cats to kangaroos.

Among the mammals, dogs belong to a specialized
group called carnivores, hunting animals that kill and
eat their prey. Scientists who study the bones and
other preserved remains of animals that lived long ago
believe that all of today's carnivores are descended
from ancestors called miacids, who lived about sixty
million years ago. The miacid probably looked much
like a present-day weasel, with a long body, short legs,
and a long, pointed snout. As the years went by—
thousands and millions of years—the miacids multi-
plied and spread. Some of them had to cope with new
conditions of life, with hot, dry deserts or steaming
jungles or chilly mountains. They found a variety of
prey animals, from mice and rabbits to deer and
sheep. The carnivores that were most successful in
adapting to the new conditions lived the longest and
left the most offspring; some of these offspring inherited the traits that had helped their parents to suc-
ceed, and they passed on these traits to their own
children.

Gradually the group of primitive carnivores separated into a number of different families, each with its
own typical appearance and way of life, each adapted
to survive in particular types of conditions. Some did
well in hot places, others developed thick coats of fur

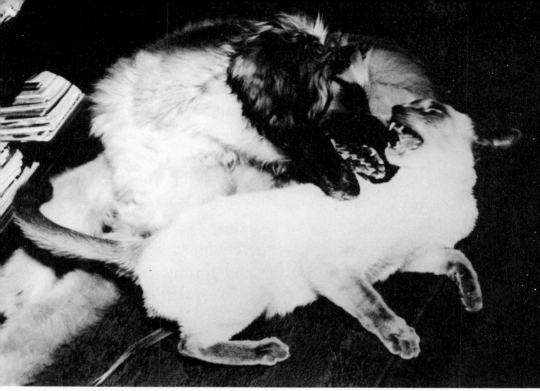

Courtesy the American Kennel Club.

This Afghan and cat at play show the carnivore habit of going for the neck.

and specialized body systems that helped them to endure severe cold. Some carnivores even adapted to life in the water and became the ancestors of our present-day seals, sea lions, and walruses. The carnivores that stayed on dry land gave rise to seven modern families: the raccoons, bears, dogs, weasels, genets, hyenas, and cats.

The miacids passed on to their carnivore descendants a number of adaptations that help in the struggle to stay alive. These include highly developed senses of smell and hearing, good for tracking and locating, and a sturdy, well-balanced skeleton and strong, tough muscles for running down the speedy and agile prey. A habit of going for the neck of the prey provided a double advantage: biting or crunching down on the delicate neck could often produce a quick kill, and meanwhile the prey was prevented from fighting back with its own teeth and jaws. The carnivore's strong jaws are equipped with some specialized teeth for tearing and cutting. All the carnivores have shearing, or knifelike, teeth in the sides of their jaws; the upper teeth slide down over the lower ones like the blades of scissors, cleanly cutting through tough meat fibers. Some of the carnivores— particularly the dogs—have four long, pointed fangs, the "canine" teeth, which are used to rip and tear.

Perhaps the most important carnivore adaptation was an increase in intelligence. A carnivore might not always be able to outrun its prey, but it could still win a dinner in the end if it could outsmart it. Thus, the brighter carnivores survived and passed on their intelligence to their offspring. A way of life that permits a teaching and sharing of experience can also be an advantage; carnivores typically have a strong bond between the mother and her children, with a fairly long period of care and training. Dogs have gone further, living in groups called packs. The pack provides a social organization, with complicated rules for finding one's place in the group and behaving suitably toward the others. The organized pack uses the hunting territory more efficiently, without wasteful competition, and indeed, the members of the pack often work together in the hunt.

The miacids first appeared on earth about fifty million years ago. The adaptations that gradually changed these ancestral carnivores into their modern descendants took a long time. It was perhaps thirty-five million years ago that the ancestors of the modern bears and those of the dogs branched off from the family tree. Weasels, cats, and other carnivore lines had already split off and were going their separate ways. The family Canidae, the "true dogs," at first included bearlike dogs, catlike dogs, and hyenalike dogs; gradually they disappeared and forms resembling our modern foxes, wolves, jackals, and dogs developed.

FROM WOLF TO *CANIS FAMILIARIS*

Dogs were the first animals domesticated by humans. There are no breeding records to tell us how this great event occurred, since it happened long before the art of writing was invented. We can never be completely sure of the details, but scientists have come up with a number of educated guesses about how it could have happened.

Stone Age humans lived as hunters and gatherers. Their hunting practices were often rather wasteful. Fossil remains show that they sometimes killed entire herds of antelope or other grazing animals, throwing stones or lighting fires to stampede them until they became bogged down in swamps or fell off cliffs. Not all these animals were butchered; many were left to rot where they fell. Probably packs of wolves roaming the same hunting territories found that it was much easier to follow the human hunters at a cautious distance and feed on their kills than to hunt and kill their own prey. But this kind of lazy life had an effect on the wolves. Even today, wolves that are caught and tamed as pups and raised in captivity grow shorter muzzles than their wild parents, and their teeth are more crowded. The same thing probably happened to the wolves who lived by scavenging the kills of Stone Age hunters. With shorter and weaker jaws, the wolves became less efficient hunters and therefore more dependent on humans. Gradually they became bolder, slipping into human camps to raid the garbage dumps and perhaps even accepting an occasional tidbit tossed by a friendly hand.

With wolves and humans living close by and sharing the same wandering, hunting way of life, it is easy to imagine how the ties between the two groups grew closer. Human hunters, finding wolf dens, may have brought some of the puppies home to raise as pets.

Courtesy Department of Library Services, American Museum of Natural History.
This young timber wolf pup could be raised for human companionship. (Photo: E.H. Baynes.)

Wolf pups can be tamed easily if they are caught young enough. The age of about three weeks is a critical period in a wolf's life; at that time its eyes are open, and it is just starting to move around actively and get acquainted with its world. This is when the pup becomes socialized, learning about the pack and all the proper wolf "manners." If it is raised by humans, the wolf pup bonds to them instead, giving them the love and devotion it would normally give to the wolves of its pack. When it grows up it remains loving and loyal to the humans who raised it. A full-grown tame wolf can be a nuisance at times—imagine having your pet wolf greet you each time you came home by leaping up to put its huge paws on your shoulders and affectionately bite your nose! But the Stone Age people found their four-legged companions very useful for guarding the camp and helping in the hunt.

Animal expert Roger Caras points out that the ancient humans may have had other motives for bringing home wolf pups. Even today, dogs are a valuable source of food in some parts of the world. Plump little wolf puppies would make a good emergency food supply for times when the hunts were unsuccessful. One can readily imagine a Stone Age child begging, "Please, can't we keep just this one?" and thus saving a favorite pup to raise as a friend and companion.

Scientists are not sure exactly where the first domestication of the dog occurred; most likely it happened in many parts of the world. Fossils of ancient dogs are found in Europe, Asia, and America, and, in fact, the oldest fossil clearly identifiable as a domesticated dog rather than a wolf or other wild canid was found in Idaho. It dates back to more than 10,500 years ago. Judging by its skeleton, this dog was closely related to the Old World dogs who arose in the Middle East, rather than to the wild canids of the New World.

It is now fairly well agreed that the main ancestor of the domestic dog was the wolf, but it seems likely that other wild canid species, including jackals and wild dogs, also contributed their genes to some of the modern dog breeds. Actually, the modern canids such as wolves, jackals, coyotes, and wild dogs are considered by scientists to be separate species, but they can interbreed with one another and with domestic dogs, and their offspring are fertile. (Normally, members of two different species cannot be bred successfully, or if they can the offspring are unable to reproduce. The mule, for example, is the sterile product of a mating between a donkey and a mare.) Not only are the various species of dogs able to interbreed, but when they have the opportunity, they often do. In areas where the territories of coyotes and wolves overlap, for instance, there are intermediate forms—wolflike coyotes and coyotelike wolves—that are apparently the result of intermatings.

Human dog breeders were not content to wait for the uncertain results of nature's matings. They soon began to experiment, arranging the matings of their dogs (or of dogs with their wild relatives) to try to bring out more desirable traits. More than ten thousand years before scientists worked out the laws of heredity, before chromosomes and genes were discovered, people were applying the laws of heredity in practice. By combining the tamest, most gentle dogs as prospective parents, they gradually bred gentler, more easily managed dogs—dogs that could learn, for example, that humans aren't really fellow wolves and don't appreciate a friendly bite on the nose as a greeting. Chance variations of color were prized and bred for, so that gradually the original wolf coat (an indistinct gray that is actually a banding of white, red, brown, and black) yielded coal-black dogs and pure white ones, dogs in various shades of red, and dogs with color patterns like black and tan. Variations of size and shape were also accentuated by dog breeders, producing an ever greater variety of breeds. Different kinds of dogs proved to be good for different purposes. Large, heavy dogs were bred to fight wild boars and other ferocious beasts, and to guard the humans and their possessions. Other large dogs were trained to pull sledges. Slim, fleet-footed dogs were bred (possibly with a little jackal in the mix) to chase after slim, fleet-footed prey such as gazelles. As cattle, sheep, and goats were domesticated, specialized

This Maremma sheepdog loafs along with the flock by day and stands guard outside the sheep pen at night.
Courtesy A.S.P.C.A.

breeds of dogs were developed to guard and herd the grazing animals. Meanwhile, the occasional dwarfs that appeared among the dog offspring were bred to chase badgers and other burrowing animals down their holes or to sit on people's laps. Gradually more and more of the breeds we know today were formed.

Large and small, no matter what their color or shape or temperament, all domestic dogs share one common trait: the ability to form a strong bond of love and loyalty with humans.

Courtesy Raymond Coppinger, Hampshire College, Amherst, Massachusetts.

A Sociable Animal

It was probably no accident that descendants of the wolf were the first animals to be domesticated by humans. Later, other wild creatures were won over and trained to carry burdens for us, to provide food and clothing, to rid our buildings of vermin, and even to share our homes. But through all those thousands of years, dogs have kept their honored position; to this day they are still the most widely kept and best loved of all the domestic animals, the one that humans can most truly regard as a friend and companion. And that was probably no accident, either. For dogs and their ancestors, the wolves, were best suited by nature to be loyal companions to humans.

WHAT DOES A DOG LOOK LIKE?

French veterinarian Fernand Mery points out that if one were to shave the fur off a hundred cats they would all wind up looking pretty much the same. Persian cats, Siamese cats, pampered show cats, wily alley cats—no matter what their breed and condition, they would all be easily recognized as cats. But if one were to shave a hundred dogs of varied breeds, what a different result there would be! Tall, slender dogs and short, stocky ones; burly giants and delicate miniatures; pointed muzzles and flat pug faces, ears and tails of all sizes and shapes—how could anyone believe that all these creatures belong to the same species?

Like their ancestor, the wolf, domestic dogs are all four-legged creatures. An inner skeleton of bones supports the dog's body, and the basic plan of the skeleton is the same for all dogs, even though the details vary from breed to breed. Inside the dog's head, the solid, heavy bones of the skull form a protective case for the brain and give shape to the jaws. The back of the skull is attached to the spine, a slender, flexible, curved tube that is formed from a long series of small bones called vertebrae, fitted together and attached by cushions of tough, shock-absorbing cartilage. The dog's spine runs from its head all the way back to the tapering end of its tail. It is neatly balanced on the four sets of leg bones, two legs in front and two behind.

A dog has the same types of bones in each leg as a human being does, but the dog's bones are somewhat differently shaped. We humans walk flat on the soles of our feet. Bears, which are fairly close carnivore relatives of the dogs, have a flat-footed walk, too. Flat feet provide stability, but they aren't built for speed. Members of the dog family have a different kind of foot. It is long and slender, with the "heel" raised, so that the dog walks on its toes. A dog has five toes on each front foot, but only four toes on each hind foot. (Some dogs have a small, incompletely developed fifth toe called a dewclaw, which does not come in contact with the ground and is not attached to the bones of the skeleton.) A dog's toes are strong and well developed, with tough, shock-absorbing cushions (pads) on the undersurface of the paw, and they are equipped with sturdy claws that help to provide a good grip on the ground. A dog's claws are shorter and blunter than a bear's, which is an adaptation for faster, more energy-efficient running. (Long, sharp claws might catch on things and slow the dog down.) While gaining this advantage, dogs have given up something: a bear can use its long, sharp claws for grasping prey, but a dog's feet are good only for walking and running; it uses its jaws for grasping. (Cats have managed to hold on to both advantages: they have long, sharp claws, good for grasping, but their claws are retractable—they can be pulled back into fleshy sheaths for walking and running. A dog's claws are not retractable; they stick out permanently.)

Domestic dogs share the same basic body plan as their wolf ancestors, but they have changed in a number of ways. A dog's muzzle is generally shorter and weaker than a wolf's. (This change may be only partly hereditary and partly due to the conditions in which the dogs live. You may recall that tame wolves, raised by humans from puppyhood, grow shorter muzzles than their wild parents; they do not have to hunt and kill their own food, and so their muzzles get less exercise.)

Even the shortest-muzzled dogs share an important trait with wolves: their noses have a lining that is richly supplied with blood vessels and specialized sense cells. We'll discuss the dog's amazing sense of

Panting is a dog's way of keeping cool.
Courtesy Mary Bloom.

smell a little later. Its nose also helps to keep its body temperature regulated. Warm-blooded animals keep their bodies at an *even* temperature—not too cold, but not too hot, either. Heat is formed as a by-product of many processes in the body, especially the movements of the muscles. If an animal did not have ways to get rid of the extra heat, it would soon be burning with fever. We humans dispose of excess heat mainly by using it to evaporate water from the sweat glands in our skin. A dog doesn't sweat when it is hot; it pants. It breathes rapidly, moving large volumes of air into and out of its lungs. The dog's entire respiratory system—from the nose and mouth down through the throat and into the lungs—has a lining rich in blood vessels that lie close to the surface. The blood carries heat away from the muscles and radiates it out through the lining of the respiratory passages, where it is carried out of the body by the quickly flowing air.

The dog and the wolf have the same basic tooth pattern: small, chisel-like cutting teeth called incisors at the front of the jaw, followed by the four long fangs called canines (one on each side, top and bottom). After that, going back along the jaw, come the premolars, which act as shearing teeth, sliding down over each other like the blades of scissors to cut through tough fibers. Finally, at the back of the jaws, are the molars: broad, heavy grinding teeth. A dog (or wolf) can crunch up bones with its molars, and it can also use them to chew vegetable foods—leaves and grains. Dogs are not nearly as carnivorous as cats, for example, and they do quite well on a mixed diet, rather than pure meat. (That was another trait that made it easy for the early wolf-dogs to adapt to life with humans, feeding on handouts of leftovers from the people's meals.) Although both dogs and wolves have the same kinds of teeth, the shorter muzzle makes the dog's teeth more crowded, and the canines are not so long and fanglike.

A dog's skull is generally somewhat smaller and rounder than a wolf's and its brain is about twenty percent smaller. Wolves and all the other kinds of wild dogs have upstanding ears, which act as sound funnels. Like antennas, they gather sound waves from the air and direct them down the ear canals into the inner ear. Most domestic dogs have lop ears: at rest their ears hang limply down, although they can be

The fanglike teeth called canines (one on each side, top and bottom) are characteristic of both dogs and wolves. (Photo: Howard W. Heitman.)

pricked up to listen to interesting sounds. (Dogs, like most other mammals, have highly developed ear muscles, which can raise, lower, and turn the outer ear flaps to make them more effective antennas. Most humans have lost this control over the outer ears, although a few of us can wiggle our ears a little.) For all of the dogs, both wild and domestic, the ears are not only organs of hearing but also organs of expression. The position of a dog's ears can communicate a great deal about its mood.

Another difference between wolves and most domesticated dogs is in the tail. The wild dog species all have a long, straight tail that tends to hang downward. But most domesticated dogs have a tail that curls upward, even at rest.

Shorter muzzle, rounder head, floppy ears, upstanding tail—those various traits have one important feature in common: they are all traits that wolves and other wild dogs exhibit *as puppies*. Some of the puppy traits may serve specific functions: the short-muzzled puppy face, for example, makes it easier for it to suckle its mother, and the down-hanging ear flaps may help to protect the delicate ear passages while the puppy is developing control over its body. But taken together, all these puppy traits serve as a sort of label, which can be read as: "This animal is young and helpless. Take care of it!" Humans find the rounded contours of a young animal cute and lovable. That is one reason that people find puppies and

Courtesy Catherine H. Brown.
The facial features of this Norfolk terrier pup say "I am helpless. Please take care of me."

kittens so appealing but then may become disenchanted when the animals lengthen out into full-grown dogs and cats. Animals, too, have an instinctive response to the typical appearance of a young animal and feel a need to care for it and protect it. Like us, they can even respond to the appeal of young animals of another species. A mother dog may accept young kittens, rabbits, or piglets and try to raise them just as though they were puppies. Dogs also respond instinctively to the helplessness of a human child. They may patiently submit to tail-pulling and other abuses from a toddler that they would never accept from an adult.

Some of the characteristics of today's domesticated dogs can probably be explained by the fact that they are puppy traits. Breeders found them appealing without realizing why and selected matings to preserve them in adult dogs. Zoologist John McLoughlin points out that barking is another puppy trait that has been preserved in most adult dogs today. Adult wolves and other wild dogs bark only when they are defending their dens, making as much noise as possible to attract attention and lead predators away. Their pups bark all the time and only gradually learn to control their barking. Human breeders bred and trained the bark into adult dogs as well, because it was a useful trait. A loudly barking dog could act as a handy alarm system, warning of all sorts of dangers, from a fire out of control to an approaching predator or even a human enemy. In addition to warning its owners, the barking dog might also frighten the intruder away.

Many of the variations among the different breeds of dogs are traits that human breeders selected for particular useful purposes. Dogs of the breed may no longer be used for the purpose for which they were originally bred, and the characteristic appearance of the breed is kept out of sentiment.

The slender, long-legged salukis were bred to chase fleet-footed antelopes and gazelles; the long body and

The long-bodied, short-legged dachshunds were originally bred for following badgers into their burrows.

short legs of the dachshund were specially selected to fit it for its job of following badgers down into their burrows.

In producing the large breeds, such as mastiffs and Saint Bernards, human breeders purposely selected the occasional "giants" that appeared among more normal-sized litters. These dogs were actually suffering from a disorder in which the growth hormone is still produced long after normal growth should have stopped. The bones become long and thick and heavy, with strong muscles and extra skin to match. Their huge size and strength fitted the mastiffs for the role of guard dogs at home and fighting dogs when their masters went to war. The enormous bulk of the Saint Bernard was useful in its work as a rescue dog.

The Aztecs of ancient Mexico bred tiny midget dogs such as the "Mexican hairless" and Chihuahua to be used as food sources. In other parts of the world, midget and dwarf dogs were bred for a different purpose: as lapdogs and "toys" to amuse the rich and the nobility. A midget dog may be bred by selecting the smallest of each litter, again and again over many generations, until a much smaller than normal but perfectly shaped miniature dog is produced. Nature sometimes provides shortcuts in the form of mutations, sudden hereditary changes, that affect the production of growth hormone. Unlike giants, who produce too much growth hormone for too long, midgets suffer from the opposite problem: their bodies stop producing the hormone before they have reached their normal size. Midget dogs are tiny, well-proportioned animals that look just like others of their breed except that they are so much smaller. Pomeranians and toy poodles are popular examples today.

Another kind of unusually small dog is the dwarf, which is also the result of a mutation. A dwarf grows in an abnormal pattern that produces a flattened face, shortened, thickened limbs, and backward-curving hips. The Pekingese is a typical example of the dwarfs in the dog world. Other dogs showing some dwarf characteristics are the Scottie, a dwarf terrier, and the basset hound, a sort of "dwarfed giant" with bloodhound ancestors.

As a typical mammal, the dog is covered with a thick coat of hair. Some dogs have sleek, smooth, short hair; others have coats with a rough, "wiry" texture; still others have fine, silky hair so long it may trail on the ground. Some of the variations are the result of whims of human breeders, but some have practical value. The dense coat of a Labrador retriever sheds water and allows it to swim through icy ponds without any discomfort. The Skye terrier, with curtains of long, silky hair falling down over its face and body, looks as though it was bred to sit on people's laps and look decorative. Actually, however, the flowing mane of hair shielded the eyes of the original Skye terriers from the prickly brambles that grow on their native island. The long, thick fur of sheepdogs and collies provides insulation against the cold in high mountain pastures.

Breeders and scientists have worked out the laws of heredity for various dog traits. If a purebred shorthaired dog is mated with a purebred longhaired dog, the puppies will be shorthaired. In genetic terms, short hair is said to be dominant and long hair is recessive (it will appear in the offspring only if both parents are carrying the genes for it). A smooth coat is dominant over a rough coat. A number of genes govern the color of dogs' coats: coal black is dominant over red (for example, the red of an Irish setter), and

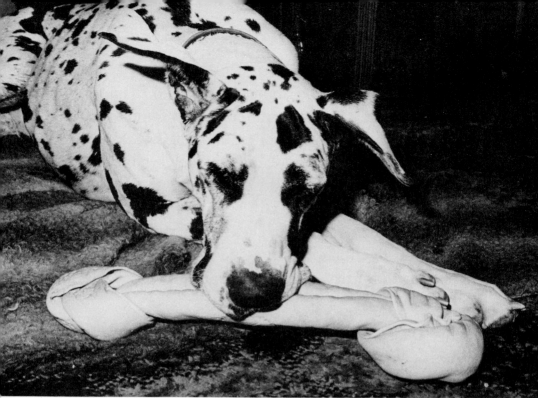

Courtesy Mary Bloom.
The spotted pattern of the Dalmatian coat is determined by genes.

red in turn is dominant over the "wild-type" coloring (the original wolf coat, which is found to some degree in domestic dogs such as the husky and the German Shepherd). The "wild-type" coloring is dominant over the black-and-tan or bicolor gene, in which the upper part of the dog's body is typically black and the lower part red, with reddish-tan markings inside the ears and above the eyes. Doberman pinschers and bloodhounds are breeds that usually have this kind of coloring.

Different series of genes can produce variations of these main color patterns or govern the patterns of spotting in black and white dogs such as Dalmatians.

Still other genes determine the size and shape of the body and head, the ears (lop ears are dominant to up-standing ears), and the pitch of a dog's bark (usually small dogs have a more high-pitched, yapping bark, while large dogs have deeper voices; one breed, the basenji, does not bark at all—it yodels). Even some aspects of dog behavior, such as pointing, retrieving, and sheepherding, are inherited in patterns just as reg-ular as those that govern the color of a dog's coat.

A DOG'S WORLD

It is hard to imagine what the world must be like, perceived by a dog. We humans are used to relying mainly on our eyes to give us a picture of everything around us. A dog's eyesight, however, is not nearly so sharp as ours. Dogs generally can barely make out an object three hundred yards away, especially if it is not moving. (Exceptions are the "gazehounds" such as the saluki, greyhound, and Afghan hound, which are bred for chasing prey over long distances and have ex-cellent eyesight. Retrievers are also keen-eyed.) Human eyes are sensitive to a whole rainbow of colors, but dogs are believed to have little if any color vision. They see the world in shades of black, grays, and browns. Dogs can see better at night than we can, though. Light that enters a dog's eye is reflected off a mirrorlike layer at the back of the eye called the tapetum. (Light from cars' headlights is reflected from the tapetum of a dog's eyes at night and makes its eyes seem to glow mysteriously.) With this extra reflecting power, even the dim shine of moonlight or starlight may give the dog enough light to see objects that we could not make out.

If a dog cannot see very well, how can it find its way around—so effectively, indeed, that dogs are trained to lead the way for blind humans? Dogs make up for their poor eyesight by an extraordinary development of other senses—one sense that humans use very little, unless they are blind, and another sense that we hardly use at all.

Dogs rely mainly on their sense of smell. Smell is a

At night, a dog's eyes can appear to glow mysteriously.
Courtesy Mary Bloom.

Courtesy the American Kennel Club.

Police dogs, such as this one, use their keen sense of smell to pursue a hidden trail.

chemical sense. Tiny chemical particles floating in the air are inhaled into the nose, where they come in contact with the moist membrane that lines the nasal passages. Some of the cells in the lining membrane are specially adapted sense cells, which recognize the shapes of particular kinds of chemicals and transmit messages to the brain. The parts of a dog's brain devoted to receiving and analyzing smell messages are much larger and better developed than the smell centers in the human brain. (But our vision center is larger and better developed than a dog's.) In fact, the dog's whole smell apparatus is much better than ours. The insides of our noses contain two postage-stamp-sized patches of sensory cells specialized for perceiving smells. The sensory area inside a dog's nose is fifteen times as large, and its sense of smell is as much as a million times as acute as ours. A dog's sense of smell is so keen that it can detect the scent of a human fingerprint made six weeks before! In Holland and Denmark, German Shepherds are used to find leaks in gas pipes. Their noses are more sensitive than most modern instruments, and they can find a break in a pipe buried several feet under a highway. Bloodhounds and other tracking dogs follow a scent trail left by microscopic particles of dead skin, which flake off whenever a person moves. In a test conducted by the New York City Police Department a few years ago, a trained bloodhound was given a sniff of a police detective's jacket and then successfully followed his trail even though the policeman had cut across an area of Central Park where a rock concert attended by fifty-five thousand people had been held the night before, passed through a meadow where nine softball games were going on, detoured onto a roadway where dozens of people from nearby apartments were walking their dogs, and then hid in some bushes. The dog found him within five minutes.

The amount of information smells can supply is limited. They can provide a trail to follow and can give a general sense of direction ("upwind" or "downwind"), but they cannot give the kind of detailed picture of the world that good eyesight provides. A dog rounds out its picture of the world with another highly developed sense: the sense of hearing. A dog's hearing is very acute, and it can hear sounds so high-pitched that we cannot hear them at all. Humans can hear sounds with frequencies up to about 30,000 cycles per second, but experiments have shown that dogs can hear sounds with frequencies up to 100,000 cycles per second. The "silent" dog whistle is an application of this difference in hearing ability: it sounds a high-pitched whistle that is beyond the limits of our ears but well within the range of a dog's hearing.

Dogs use sounds to help to locate objects, determining if a particular sound is closer to one ear than to the other. The dog typically "pricks up its ears" to listen, and its ears act as effective antennas, fine-tuning the pickup and funneling the sounds down into the inner ears where the specialized sense cells are located.

Dogs use all three senses—smell, hearing, and sight—to communicate. The sense of smell is the most important. A dog comes equipped with a whole assortment of scent-producing glands that it uses to communicate with other dogs. The odorous chemicals are called pheromones; some of them are strong-smelling to humans, while others aren't noticeable to us but are very interesting to another dog. Between the pads of a dog's paws are little glandular pockets used to mark the trail as the dog walks or runs. Other dogs, sniffing the ground, can follow such a pheromone trail hours or even days later. At the top of the base of the tail there is a scent gland that provides information about the dog's sexual status. (In foxes this gland is called the "violet gland" because of the distinctive odor it produces.) When two dogs meet, they sniff each other's tail regions. Humans may find that behavior a bit embarrassing, but to the dogs it makes good sense: they are exchanging all sorts of interesting and useful information. Glands next to the anus put scent markers on a dog's feces, for the information of other dogs who might happen to pass by. Still other scent glands pour pheromones into the dog's urine. While roaming around its territory, a dog pauses now and then to mark a tree trunk, a rock, or some other landmark with urine. Other dogs can read the urine markers to discover exactly which dog passed by, its sex, its age, and even its mood at the time. (The "scent of fear" can warn other dogs of possible trouble ahead.) In addition to the specialized sense cells in its nose, the dog has two small openings in the roof of its mouth containing sense organs for taste. A dog that has found an interesting scent wrinkles its nose, curls its lips, and bares its teeth so that it can draw air into the mouth, too. Sampling the scents, it "tastes" the air in a movement that scientists call by the German word *flehmen*. It looks rather like a silly smile.

Sounds provide another means of communication for dogs. Except for yodeling basenjis, domestic dogs have a vocal repertoire that includes barking, a wolflike howl, a low growl, and a whine. Wolves give voice to melodious howls and may serenade the moon or hold long-distance conversations with other wolves for hours. Their domesticated descendants conduct their conversations, both with other dogs and with humans, by way of barking. Each breed has its own distinctive bark, although the voices of individual dogs may also vary within a particular breed. Puppies tend to have higher-pitched barks, even when they belong to a breed that barks in a deep "Woof!" as adults. A low-pitched, rumbling growl is a warning, a sign of hostility. A dog's whine is a distress call, especially when it is left alone or confined, and it is generally directed at humans rather than at other dogs. The experts' opinions are somewhat divided on the subject of what a dog's howling means. Dogs howl during the mating season, and this vocalizing may be part of their courtship or perhaps an announcement to the canine world that they are available. But sometimes howling seems to be an expression of deep distress: a dog left alone may progress from whining to mournful howling, and there have been many reports of a dog howling beside the body of its dead master. Certain sounds, such as fire sirens and high-pitched music, can set dogs off howling in accompaniment. Pet owners may insist that their dog is trying to "sing along." Some experts have claimed that particular sounds may hurt the dog's sensitive ears; others say that they resemble sounds of the mating call, and the

48

dog mistakes the siren for a sex object. Presumably the dogs know why they are howling, but so far they haven't been able to find a way to tell us.

Dogs' sight may be generally weak, but they do use some visual means of communicating. A dog's posture gives other dogs important clues about its mood. The ears provide one set of signals. When a dog's ears are erect, it is alert and playful. If its ears are cocked to the side, watch out—it's in a challenging mood. A dog with its ears flat and folded back is signaling the opposite: it is defensive and submissive, ready to give way without a fight.

A dog's tail is another signal flag. Everybody "knows" that a wagging tail means a dog is friendly. But not everybody realizes that there is much more to the tail story and that not every wag is a friendly invitation to play. A dog with its tail held low is feeling insecure and submissive; if the tail is between its legs, it is downright afraid. A tail held low and wagging signals friendly submission. A tail held high and stiff is a danger flag: if the dog's tail isn't moving, it is alert and may be threatening; if the tail is moving slightly, the dog is feeling unsure; and if the high, stiff tail is wagging, that is a challenge. But a high tail waving gracefully back and forth means that the dog is playful and excited.

The dog's mouth provides still another set of cues. A friendly dog will extend its tongue straight out and lick your face. Dogs greet each other that way, too.

This dog may be signalling with its tongue that it is worried or frightened. (Photo: Stan Schenfeld.)

But a dog that is making small licking motions with its tongue curled back toward its nose is worried or frightened; if you try to approach it, it may bite. A dog that looks as if it is smiling is probably sampling the air for interesting scents. But if the lips are drawn back and trembling, exposing the teeth, that is a threat. Deep growls may make the threat even more frightening and effective, but the shrewd dog-watcher knows that if a dog with its lips drawn back is not growling, that may be even worse—it is the last sign of defiance before the dog attacks.

When a dog rolls over on its back and lies there, belly up, with its feet cocked in the air, that is the ultimate sign of surrender. Wild dogs use this posture

This military police dog at the Army base in Fort Bragg, North Carolina, shows its playful side. (Photo: Sgt. Lori Goodrow.)
Courtesy U.S. Army.

to show their submissiveness to the leader of the pack: they are showing their trust by offering him their belly, the softest, most vulnerable part of the body. Domestic dogs may roll over this way to greet their owner, showing their submissiveness to the human who is the leader of their home "pack." The human responds with a friendly belly rub, and the dog wriggles and whimpers its delight at being accepted again.

A DOG'S LIFE

Researchers at the Canine Psychology Center in Bar Harbor, Maine, have been studying a colony of dogs of various ages and breeds that live together under "natural" conditions, with a minimum of interference from humans. The researchers have found that in this situation domesticated dogs form a pattern of life very similar to that of their wolf ancestors. They hunt together and live in harmony in a community called a pack, each one knowing its own place in the group and giving loyalty and respect to the pack leader. The leader is the strongest, smartest, ablest member of the pack, and his job is to command, guide, watch over, punish, and protect the others. The pack leader wins his position by challenging and fighting the old leader; he holds on to his leadership only as long as he can successfully face the challenges of other ambitious dogs in the group. Within the pack there are continual challenges and struggles for position. Sometimes these lead to real fights (though not usually to the point of serious injuries). More often they are a matter of threats and bluffs, with both dogs acting their most ferocious until one of them rolls over in the belly-up gesture of submission. Dogs are generally good losers and gracious winners: even in the heat of a real dogfight, the belly-up surrender will bring a prompt acceptance from the winner. The fight stops, and the two dogs are friends again.

When dogs live with humans, they seem to view the human family as their pack, and they give their loyalty and allegiance to the master who feeds and protects them.

As hunting animals, wild canids stake out a home territory that they consider their own personal domain. They patrol the boundaries of their territory, carefully marking them by rubbing against trees or scratching the bark, by urinating, and by leaving their droppings. The pheromones in the urine and feces act as chemical "No Trespassing" signs, warning other canids that the territory is already occupied.

Domestic dogs have kept this sense of territory. Usually they take the boundaries of their master's property as their home ground. A dog being taken for a walk will tend to relieve itself in the same places each time, leaving its marks to announce its presence to the world. When a dog's territory is invaded—by a dog, another animal, or a human—it will bark a challenge. If the warning is ignored, the dog may attack. How aggressively a dog will defend its territory depends on its training, its breed, and whether it is restrained. A large dog might seem more menacing, but actually many of the small breeds are more aggressive: a yapping Pomeranian, refusing to yield an inch, might send a huge boxer cringing in retreat. A dog roaming free may content itself with a few warning barks at intruders, whereas a dog that is chained may become angry or frightened. (If a stranger walks inside the range of a dog's chain, the dog may become so upset that it attacks. This is especially likely if the intruder turns his back, thus stimulating a chasing reflex.) Dogs in groups tend to be bolder and more aggressive than the same dogs on their own.

On our daily walks down a country lane we have plenty of opportunity to observe the varied habits of dogs defending their territory. Most of our neighbors have dogs; some obey the local "leash laws," but others do not. The first dogs on our route are two Shetland sheepdogs. They are usually indoors, but if they are out they are content with an alert posture and a few barks; a call from their mistress or master brings them scampering back home. Then come a German Shepherd and a Labrador penned together in a fenced-in run while their master is at work. Passing their property brings a chorus of barks and howling, even though we keep to the road. An aggressive little poodle at the next house puts up a bold front but is a coward at heart. He paces us from one end of the property to the other, staying carefully on his master's grass while we walk on the roadway, and barking aggressively. When we call him by name and hold out a hand to sniff, he stops barking and backs away warily; if we move toward him, he turns tail and runs back home. The springer spaniel two houses down should know us by now, too, but he usually comes dashing out to the edge of the road, barking, and watches us carefully until we are out of his territory. He, too, generally stays on the grass. At the bottom of the lane there is a chorus of barks from the dachshunds in their kennel; they can't see the road, but they hear us coming. On the way back home, we murmur silent thanks that our former next-door neighbors have moved away. They had four dogs: an aggressive little mongrel, a part malamute with a reputation for biting, a golden retriever that was supposedly being raised as a Seeing-Eye dog but was later rejected, and a large black German Shepherd. Despite repeated complaints, those dogs were allowed to run free, terrorizing the neighbors. When we passed, they not only barked furiously but sometimes dashed right out onto the road at us. (We usually walked past that part of the road sideways, looking as brave as possible.) Finally, as we approach our house, there is our own part-Lab mutt, Jacqui, leaping at the end of her sliding chain and wagging her tail furiously in greeting. Jacqui doesn't bark at us, but she does bark at deer, woodchucks, repairmen, the UPS driver, and any other strangers who invade her territory.

Defense of a territory is only one of the many types of aggressive behavior that dogs may display. Predatory aggression is the kind that occurs when a dog chases a rabbit or a cat. (Our cats have a habit of walking about one foot beyond the reach of Jacqui's chain. One day her lunges broke the rope along which the chain slides, and she went dashing after the surprised cat. She didn't catch it though.) Aggression in dogs may be the result of fear. That is the explanation for many attacks on children. The child comes rushing up to a strange dog with his or her hand out to pat it; the dog misunderstands the gesture, is frightened, and bites. Male dogs may fight in a kind of sexual competition; females may become aggressive when they are defending a litter of puppies. When a family has more than one dog, they may fight in competition for food or for their owner's affection. Among wild dogs, this kind of dispute would quickly sort itself out and one of the dogs would make a submissive gesture. But humans tend to interfere, trying to protect the weaker dog, and may just prolong the problem.

When two dogs meet, they greet each other with sniffings of the tail region, where various pheromone-producing glands are located. Getting acquainted in this way may lead to friendship or even—at certain times of the year—to the dog's version of romance. A male dog is ready to mate at any time, but a female

56

dog (called a bitch) is receptive only when she is in season, usually about twice a year. Her sex organs pass through a cycle of preparation for mating called heat. At the beginning of the cycle, her body begins to produce pheromones, which are carried through the air and attract males from far and wide. For the first week or so she will refuse her suitors, even though they will sniff each other interestedly. Then tiny eggs are released from her ovaries, and she becomes receptive to mating. The bitch will continue to accept males for three to five days after the start of her receptive period.

The mating of dogs starts with a courtship. First comes the sniffing by which dogs get acquainted. Then the dogs may appear to fight, but they are only playing at aggression. Finally the bitch signals her readiness by standing with her tail held to the side. The male mounts her and deposits a fluid containing sperm inside her body. The microscopic sperm look like tiny tadpoles. They swim up to meet the eggs and may join with them; each pair of sperm and egg that join may start the life of a puppy.

There are some things about dogs' mating behavior that may upset humans who observe them. First of all, dogs do not remain faithful to a single mate but instead will cheerfully take advantage of whatever sexual opportunities may arise. A bitch in heat may attract a whole crowd of eager swains who follow her for hours on end and try to mount her as soon as she stops to catch her breath. Eventually, when she is ready, she chooses one (or merely accepts the male who is nearest or the most persistent). When she mates again, she may choose a different male, and in her period of heat she may mate with a whole series of males. (It is possible for a single litter to include puppies with several different fathers. But there is no truth to the old belief that if a purebred bitch mates with a mongrel, she will be "spoiled" for life and all her later litters will be mongrels too. The puppies in one litter will have no effect on those in later litters.)

Sometimes during mating, the two dogs may remain joined together for as much as thirty to forty minutes. The male is locked in tight and cannot free himself without great pain. The sight of two dogs joined together end-to-end for half an hour may be comical or upsetting, depending on your viewpoint, but it is perfectly normal and there is no need to do anything about it. Eventually they will come apart.

Dog owners may also worry when a male dog tries persistently to mount another male. That is apparently due to a little mix-up in the pheromone signals. It's common and nothing to worry about; it doesn't mean that the dog is "gay."

Puppies develop inside their mother's body for about sixty-three days. Near the end of the pregnancy, the mother dog may become restless and roam about, looking for a nest site. She may make digging movements (even on the solid floors of the house) and may tear up papers. Some dogs will accept a nest box lined with soft rags prepared by their owner; others may have their puppies right out in the middle of the floor.

The puppies are usually born one at a time, about twenty to sixty minutes apart. Each one comes out of its mother's body wrapped all over in a thin membrane like a plastic bag. The mother tears the membrane open with her mouth and licks it away. She continues to lick the puppy until it is clean and then bites off its umbilical cord and eats the afterbirth. (The afterbirth looks like a small piece of raw liver. It was the connection to the mother's body and supplied the puppy with nourishment through the umbilical cord connected to the puppy's belly.)

A newborn puppy is blind and deaf and almost helpless. But it can crawl, and with its mother helpfully nudging it along, it can find one of the teats on her belly and begin to suck. Rich milk, produced inside the mother dog's body, pours out through her teats. The milk formed during the first twenty-four hours after the puppies' birth has an extra bonus: a substance called colostrum, which gives the puppies protection against diseases such as distemper. At first the mother stays in the nest almost all the time, cuddling her puppies to keep them warm and feeding them every few hours. She leaves the nest only for brief periods, to eat or to relieve herself.

Gradually, as the puppies grow, their mother

Courtesy Mary Bloom.
This seven-day-old pup is almost totally helpless.

begins to leave them for longer periods. By the time they are two weeks old, she may be gone for two or three hours at a time. At this age the puppies' eyes are opening, although they cannot see very well yet, and they are starting to become active.

By three weeks the puppies can walk. They can see well and can hear sounds. (A loud sound may startle them.) Soon they begin to play, pulling on their mother's ears and tail and batting and nipping each other.

At four to five weeks, when the puppies are scampering about actively, the mother begins to produce less milk and she may become annoyed at the tugs and nips on her teats. Her puppies are ready for weaning. The mother dog begins introducing them to solid food. She eats her own meal and then vomits up globs of partly digested food for her pups to eat. That may seem like a rather disgusting practice, but it is effective: it provides the growing puppies with soft, easy-to-digest "baby food." (The dog's owner may start the weaning process with meals of Pablum and formula or strained baby meats.) Within a week or two the puppies can graduate to regular food—a commercial puppy chow or a mashed-up mixture of chopped meat, vegetables, and cereal.

Researchers who have studied dog behavior have found that the best time to take puppies away from their mother is at six to eight weeks. If they are taken away earlier, they may become too dependent and attached to humans and will not be able to get along well with other dogs. On the other hand, if puppies do not have any contact with humans until thirteen weeks, they become fearful of humans and almost impossible to train.

After weaning, the puppies continue to grow rap-

Courtesy Ruth F. Almstedt.
The best time for these beagle pups to be weaned from their mother is from six to eight weeks of age.

idly. They are very curious and mischievous and full of energy. Gradually, though, they start to calm down and can be housebroken and trained to obey simple commands. At six to eight months a female dog has her first cycle of heat, and a male begins to lift his hind leg when he urinates. Now the dog is sexually mature (able to mate), although it may not reach its full growth until it is about a year old. Depending on the breed, a dog's life span is from about ten to fifteen years.

DO DOGS HAVE ESP?

In the thousands of years that people have been living with dogs, an amazing rapport has grown between our two species. Humans can learn to interpret their dogs' varied barks, growls, and whines, as well as their postures and gestures. Dogs can learn to recognize and understand a limited number of human words. (They seem to rely both on the sound of the words and on the tone of voice.) They are also adept at guessing their owners' moods from clues of posture, voice, expression, and even odors. (We produce some pheromones, too.) Sometimes a dog's understanding seems almost psychic, as though it were capable of mind reading; but keen observation, using its senses of sight, smell, and hearing, can probably explain this uncanny rapport. And yet, there have been many curious incidents involving dogs that have led some people to suggest that they may have senses that we do not possess or may even be able to use some sort of extrasensory perception—ESP.

Several minutes before the first tremors of an earthquake are felt, the dogs in the area become restless: they tremble, bark, and howl. Scientists believe that they may be sensitive to tiny shivers in the ground, too slight for us to perceive; or perhaps to changes in the smell of the ground caused by gases released in the quake; or perhaps to storms in the earth's magnetic field.

Sometimes a dog sitting peacefully will suddenly leap up and begin to race around wildly, barking; or it may stand up and back away, growling, with teeth bared, as though it is confronting an enemy. Yet there seems to be nothing there. In more superstitious times, people believed that there were ghosts or spirits roaming about, which could be seen by dogs but not by humans. Today we have more scientific explanations for such incidents. Perhaps the dog is reacting to a distant sound or a whiff of odor that happened to waft by. Or the dog may be acting out its confused reactions to a fragment of a dream or a daydream. For the past few decades, researchers have been studying sleep in humans and animals by attaching electrodes to their heads and recording the patterns of electricity that pulse through their brains. (The amount of electricity generated by a brain is very small, but delicate instruments can amplify and record it.) Sleep researchers have found that typical sleep includes periods of deep sleep, when the brain waves trace out long, slow, even waves; and periods when the brain waves look very much like the typical patterns from the waking state even though the person or animal is sound asleep. That phase of sleep is referred to as "paradoxical sleep," because of the contradiction between the brain-wave patterns and the sleeping state. Humans wakened during this phase of sleep almost always report that they are dreaming and may describe the events of the dream in vivid detail. Animals in paradoxical sleep cannot tell us what is going through their minds, but they certainly look as though they are dreaming. A sleeping dog may twitch, whimper, or bark; its tail may thump against the floor; and its paws may make running motions. Watching it, you can imagine it sniffing along an odor trail or chasing a rabbit or defending its territory from a menacing mailman. Researchers have even produced dreams at will: when they held a piece of strong-smelling sausage about three inches from a sleeping dog's nose, for example, it promptly began to make chewing movements even though it was still sound asleep.

Still another mystery of the dog world is their homing ability. In scientific tests, dogs do not do as well in finding their way back home as pigeons, cats, or various other animals. But in real life there have been some amazing incidents. In one recent case a teenaged boy adopted a mixed-breed dog from an animal shelter in Ohio and named him Rocky. A month later the boy moved to Arkansas to work on a ranch and took Rocky along with him. After a few months, the teenager quit his job and went back home to Ohio by bus. He left Rocky with friends, intending to save up enough money to send for him. But the dog had other ideas. He disappeared right after his master left. Nearly six months later a family in Ohio found a stray dog wandering around. The dog seemed friendly, and he had a license tag attached to his collar. A check

Courtesy Robert Burden.

This statue in New York's Central Park of the sled dog, Balto, is dedicated to the "indominatable spirit" of the one hundred and fifty sled dogs that carried a package of diphtheria antitoxin over a nearly 700-mile trail from Nenana to Nome, Alaska. Balto led the sled team on the final lap, sniffing and feeling his way along the trail made invisible by an eighty-mile-an-hour snowstorm.

with the county sheriff's department gave them the name of the dog's owner. Soon Rocky and his master were reunited. The dog, on his own, had traveled 824 miles on his trip back home.

Various explanations have been offered for dogs' amazing ability to find their way home. Perhaps the dog, anxious and upset by the separation from its owner, sets out at random and then happens upon a familiar scent or noise or landmark that it recalls from previous trips. It uses these landmarks as a guide, sometimes blundering and then getting back on track by a continuing process of trial and error. This explanation could account for a short trip over terrain familiar to the dog. But what about a long journey like Rocky's? On the trip from Ohio to Arkansas he had traveled by car and so had never had a chance to see or smell most of the route. Perhaps in such cases the dog navigates by the stars or by the position of the sun in the sky. Perhaps it can sense the flow of the earth's magnetic field and use that as a navigating guide. These are explanations that have been suggested for the long flights of migrating birds, and they could explain most of the reported cases of homing dogs, too. But a few cases remain unexplained.

The Dog Breeds

People have been breeding dogs for thousands of years, tinkering with the canid genes and molding shapes and sizes, colors, even personality and instincts. Dog breeding could even be thought of as an art form, like sculpture, with dogs a kind of modeling clay that obligingly shapes itself to match human needs and fancies. Some of today's dog breeds are very old, descended virtually unchanged from ancient times. Others date back less than a century. Breeds come and go in popularity: the cocker spaniel was America's top dog for a time, but now it has dropped behind the poodle. When a dog breed falls completely out of favor, it may become extinct, disappearing within about fifteen years.

Standards for dog breeds are set by organizations like the American Kennel Club, which currently registers 127 breeds of dogs. The standards are maintained by careful choices of matings. Each registered purebred dog has a pedigree, a detailed history of its ancestry that goes back over many generations. Breeders examine the pedigrees of prospective sires (the male parents) and dams (the female parents) to find combinations that are likely to produce desirable characteristics in the offspring. Some of the breeding standards govern the dog's appearance—size, shape of the head, body, and tail, color and markings, texture of the coat, and so forth. There may also be standards for the dog's gait (the way it moves) and its temperament.

Dog breeding today can be not only an art but also a lucrative business. Friends of ours have recently obtained a mate for their purebred bulldog and are eagerly looking forward to breeding the pair. Breeding bulldogs can be difficult and expensive: the puppies generally cannot be born normally because of their large heads and must be delivered by a cesarean operation. But it will be worth the effort: pedigreed bulldog puppies are selling these days for $800 to $1,200 each!

Despite the great variations among breeds, from tiny Chihuahuas to huge Saint Bernards and Great Danes, all dogs still have a basic set of *Canis familiaris* genes. Animal expert Roger Caras points out that if a couple dozen dogs of different breeds were put together in a very large pen and allowed to breed freely for a dozen years or so, you would come back to find that the youngest generation was tending toward

70

a sort of general, all-purpose "universal dog." It would weigh about thirty to forty pounds and have light bones, a small head with upstanding ears, and dainty feet. Its coat would be gray to brown, and its brushy tail would curve out and down or perhaps up and over. Also roaming around the pen would be the middle generations—more recognizable intermediate forms, crosses between two or three breeds. All but the original purebred parents would be mixed-breed or "random-bred" dogs, commonly referred to as mongrels or mutts.

The various breeds of dogs recognized today can be classified into groups according to their ancestry and the purposes for which they were bred. The American Kennel Club divides them into seven main groups:

Sporting dogs	Terriers
Hounds	Toys
Working dogs	Non-sporting dogs
Herding dogs	

Objections have been made to various parts of this classification. Some "working dogs," for example, no longer work, and the sporting instincts have long since been bred out of some of the "sporting dogs." Roger Caras believes that the "non-sporting" group should be renamed "companion dogs," and some dogs currently listed in other groups, such as the basenji, cocker spaniel, dachshund, miniature schnauzer, Norwegian elkhound, and pug, should be added to the companion group. These suggestions seem reasonable, but at present the American Kennel Club classification is the most widely accepted.

SPORTING DOGS

The sporting group consists mainly of the pointers, retrievers, setters, and spaniels and includes a total of twenty-four breeds:

Pointer
Pointer, German short-
  haired
Pointer, German wire-
  haired
Retriever, Chesapeake Bay
Retriever, curly-coated
Retriever, flat-coated
Retriever, golden
Retriever, Labrador
Setter, English
Setter, Gordon
Setter, Irish
Spaniel, American water

Spaniel, Brittany
Spaniel, Clumber
Spaniel, cocker
Spaniel, English cocker
Spaniel, English springer
Spaniel, field
Spaniel, Irish water
Spaniel, Sussex
Spaniel, Welsh springer
Vizsla
Weimaraner
Wirehaired pointing grif-
  fon

The hunting specialty of pointers is obvious from their name: their job is to find game and then to "point," standing absolutely motionless and staring at the prey to show the hunter its location. The pointer breeds go back several hundred years. In the mid-1600s, when they were first bred, pointers were used to locate and point hares, and then hunting greyhounds were unleashed to catch them. By the early

This German shorthaired pointer demonstrates the position for which it is named.

1700s, shooting came into fashion, and hunters with guns shot the game that their dogs pointed out. Pointers are graceful dogs, muscular without being too heavy, and full of energy. They develop more rapidly than most dog breeds: by two months, pointer puppies are already showing a keen interest in small game and instinctively take the pointing position with neck stretched forward, tail out stiff behind, and standing on three legs with one foreleg bent at the knee joint.

While pointing, the dog shows enormous concentration, standing motionless for minutes at a time almost as though it were in a trance. One tall tale told in Victorian times claimed that a hunter lost his pointer on the moors, and a year later he found the skeleton of the dog still pointing at the skeleton of a bird. The story wasn't true, of course, but it does capture the spirit of the dog.

Retrievers specialize in bringing back the hunter's prey after it has been killed on the wing. Retrievers have excellent eyesight and an amazing ability to track the path of a falling bird and estimate where it will land. Protected by a dense, water-shedding coat, the dog does not hesitate to swim through the iciest waters to fetch the prey. It carries the bird very gently, without biting or crushing it, and brings it back undamaged to its master. (Our part-Labrador, Jacqui, adores fetching sticks and carrying around stuffed toys, held by the neck in her jaws. But she can't seem to catch on to the other half of the job: she'll retrieve things and bring them to us, but then she refuses to give them up. We're not sure whether the problem is that she doesn't have a full set of Labrador retriever genes, or that she just hasn't been fully trained. She's still young, so we'll keep trying.) The Labrador retriever actually comes from Newfoundland rather than Labrador. It dates back to the early 1800s, and its short coat can come in the typical coal black or in yellow or chocolate. Golden retrievers were developed somewhat later in the nineteenth century; they are longer-haired and have some spaniel in their ancestry.

Setters were developed in England more than four hundred years ago. In those days, birds were often caught with nets. The setter's job was to find the game, point it out, and then keep out of the way while the hunters cast their nets. So the setters were trained to "set," or crouch low to the ground. The English setter is the oldest of the setter breeds. It has a long, lean head and a muscular body, and its coat is often white spotted with one or more colors. The Irish setter, with its long, elegant body and rich mahogany or chestnut red coat, has long been a favorite of artists, many of whom have called it the most beautiful of all dogs.

The spaniels' name comes from "dog of Spain," the country where they are thought to have originated. Spaniels are among the oldest breeds of hunting dogs. References to them in writings from the fourteenth century mention that they were already divided into two groups, water and land spaniels. Water spaniels were used to retrieve game in duck hunting; land spaniels tracked game birds by scent and then flushed them out of their cover in the thick brush so that the hunters could see and net them. When hunting with guns became popular, spaniels tracked and flushed out game, stayed motionless while the gun was fired, and then retrieved the birds. Some of the land spaniels were "springers," who worked by springing on a variety of game to flush them up for the hunters. Smaller varieties specialized in work on woodcocks and were called cocking or "cocker" spaniels. By the end of the nineteenth century, separate springer and cocker breeds had been developed. Meanwhile, small toy varieties of the spaniel were bred as lapdogs. Today the American cocker spaniel is not really a hunting dog. Toward the end of the last century it became a favorite among pet owners and was bred so widely to satisfy the demand that it lost many of its hunting instincts.

The vizsla is a pointer bred in Hungary, with a long history going back at least a thousand years. Drawings from that period, at the time of the Magyar invasions of Hungary, show vizsla-like dogs being used with falcons to hunt game birds. Writings from the fourteenth century indicate that dog breeders were careful to keep the bloodlines of these hunting dogs pure.

The weimaraner is a pointer that was bred in Germany in the early nineteenth century by crossing bloodhounds with German hunting dogs. Its gray color and its silent, effortless movements have given it the nickname of "Gray Ghost." It works best and is happiest when it is living with a human family, rather than in a kennel with other dogs.

The sporting dogs, with their patient, obedient dispositions, make excellent pets, but they require a great deal of exercise. If they are not able to work off excess energy and use their hunting instincts, they may develop dangerous habits, such as chasing cars.

HOUNDS

The hound group includes some of the most ancient of all the dog breeds. The twenty currently recognized breeds in this group are:

Afghan hound	Greyhound
Basenji	Harrier
Basset hound	Ibizan hound
Beagle	Irish wolfhound
Black-and-tan coonhound	Norwegian elkhound
Bloodhound	Otter hound
Borzoi	Rhodesian Ridgeback
Dachshund	Saluki
Foxhound, American	Scottish deerhound
Foxhound, English	Whippet

The hounds are hunting dogs. Unlike the sporting dogs, which are used to find or flush out game for human hunters to shoot or snare, and to retrieve it afterward, the hounds themselves are generally the hunters' weapons—splendid hunting machines that can track their prey by scent or sight and then catch and kill it.

The basenji is a bit of an oddity in the hound group. In fact, it is a bit of an oddity among dogs in general. It is a very ancient breed, one of the most ancient of all the pure breeds. Pictures of basenjis are found in Egyptian art five thousand years old. These dogs are pictured as pets in household settings, although natives of central Africa today use them for pointing, flushing, and retrieving game, and for hunting reed rats. Basenjis are apparently descended from the same ancestors as the half-wild pariah dogs that roam the cities and towns of India, Asia Minor, and northern Africa. Their variable coloring and curly

Notice the erect ears, a breed characteristic, of this three-month-old basenji puppy.

Courtesy the American Kennel Club.

tails indicate that the pariah dogs were once domesticated and bred by humans. But now they live in packs as scavengers, scrounging scraps of garbage and even eating corpses. They serve a useful function in areas where sanitation is primitive and help to stop the spread of disease. But many peoples have treated them as outcasts: Hindus and Muslims regard dogs as unclean, and the ancient Hebrews called the eating of dog flesh an "abomination."

Basenjis are smaller than pariah dogs—an average male stands seventeen inches at the shoulder and weighs twenty-four pounds—and it would be rather an insult to call them "unclean." In fact, basenjis are quite fussy about their personal cleanliness and continually wash and groom themselves like a housecat. Basenjis are known as "barkless dogs." Normally they are silent, unless they have been taught to bark by dogs of other breeds; when a basenji is happy, it gives voice to a sort of chortling yodel. Playful and gentle, the basenji has an endearing habit of sweeping its paw from behind one ear down over the tip of its nose. It repeats this movement over and over again until it has gained its owner's attention. (This play-invitation gesture is a behavior trait shared by other breeds with erect ears, including German Shepherds, huskies, and malamutes.)

The saluki, the royal dog of Egypt, is another very ancient breed of dog. Pictures of salukis appear on Egyptian tombs from about 2100 B.C., and very similar dogs are depicted in carvings from an even older Sumerian empire, which may date back to 7000–6000 B.C. Salukis were mummified and placed with honor in tombs, like the Egyptian pharaohs themselves. Mentions of "dogs" in the Bible apparently refer to salukis, and even the Muslims, who regarded dogs in general as unclean, made an exception for the saluki, declaring it sacred and calling it "the noble one," a gift of Allah. (That way they could eat the prey brought down by their hunting salukis.)

Salukis are typical "gazehounds," or sight hounds. They have large protruding eyes and keen eyesight. Their bodies are built for speed: long, slim, with powerful legs and a marvelously efficient cooling mechanism in the cavities of the nose and sinuses. The wolf, the saluki's ancestor, runs on thick, heavy-muscled legs, but breeders of the gazehounds have streamlined all the extra weight off their lower legs and concentrated their running muscles in the upper legs and lower backs. They run in a series of almost rabbitlike leaps, with the long spine flexing and unflexing like a steel spring. The greyhound, another Egyptian dog that dates back at least five thousand years; the whippet, an English miniature greyhound a little more than a century old; the saluki; and the Afghan hound, the "royal hunting dog of Afghanistan," are all typical gazehounds. They all have the same basic greyhound body type, but the greyhound and whippet are shorthaired, while the saluki has a feathering of longer

Courtesy the American Kennel Club.
The long, slim, powerful legs of the greyhound are ideally suited for high-speed running.

hair on its ears, legs, and tail, and the Afghan hound is covered on all but its pointed face with long, thick, silky hair. Gazehounds have a very strong chasing instinct, tending to take off after anything that moves. They are so excitable that ancient humans often kept them hooded, like falcons, until the prey was sighted.

In northern Europe, gazehound blood was bred into hunting dogs and produced the Irish wolfhound (the tallest dog in the world), the Scottish deerhound, and the borzoi, or "Russian wolfhound." All these dogs are basically greyhound types with long, thick fur to keep them warm in the more northern climate. (The shorthaired whippets, on the other hand, have virtually no protection from the cold. When they are kept as pets, they demand a blanket of their own to roll into whenever they feel chilly; if their owner doesn't supply one, they will cheerfully help themselves to the family's bedspreads.)

When gazehounds are kept as pets, they need a great deal of exercise and attention. The owner learns to keep a firm grip on the dog's leash at all times when it is out for an airing; otherwise, the dog may suddenly take off on one of its lightning dashes and disappear.

While gazehounds depend on their eyesight, scent hounds have developed the nose to perfection. The champion sniffer in the dog world is the bloodhound. This large, sturdy dog was well known in the Mediterranean countries more than two thousand years ago and was brought to continental Europe and England before the time of the Crusades. The folds of loose skin that give the bloodhound's face such a mournful expression help it to work its way loose from prickly brambles when it is following a scent through thick underbrush. It uses its floppy ears to stir up the dust along its way, making scent-filled particles swirl up to its sensitive nose. A bloodhound on the hunt is single-minded, following the scent silently and tirelessly. In fact, when bloodhounds are used to track lost children or escaped criminals, they are always kept on a lead—not only because they might quickly leave their handler behind if they were free but also because a bloodhound has no road sense. Left on its own, it would keep on following the interesting scent and blunder heedlessly into the path of oncoming cars on the first roadway it came to.

People imagine that the bloodhound got its name from its bloodthirsty hunting practices. Nothing could be further from the truth. The bloodhound is a very gentle and affectionate dog, and when it reaches its quarry it is more likely to deliver a friendly lick than a bite. Most likely the name came from the fact that in past centuries only the rich and noble—the "blue bloods"—were permitted to own the best scent hounds. These dogs were thus called "hounds of the blood," "blooded hounds," or "bloodhounds." Bloodhounds have been used to track criminals for a long time. An English law of 1527 stated that anyone denying entrance to a "sleuth hound" became an accessory to the crime, and another old English law said that if a bloodhound led its handlers to someone's door, that was as good as a search warrant. Even today a bloodhound's "testimony" is admissible as evidence in court.

Other keen-nosed scent hounds are the beagle, basset, and dachshund. Beagles are an old breed, dating to before the time of the ancient Greeks and Romans. They closely resemble the original hound ancestors

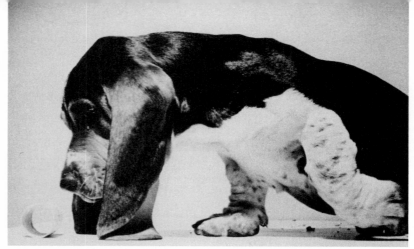

Basset hound puppies often trip over their long ears when they run.

and are often used in packs for hunting. The basset hound is a long, low dog with very heavy bones. Its name comes from the French *bas*, meaning "low" or "dwarf." The basset's nose is second only to the bloodhound's, and it hunts alone or in packs. Its gentle disposition makes it a good house pet.

The dachshund is so long-bodied and short-legged that it looks like a caricature. Its odd shape was not the result of human whims but was bred for a special purpose. In the fifteenth, sixteenth, and seventeenth centuries, dachshunds were used to hunt badgers, following them right down into their burrows. (The dachshund's name comes from German words meaning "badger dog.") The badger-hunting dachshunds were strong, sturdy, courageous dogs, weighing up to thirty or thirty-five pounds and well able to hold their own against the vicious attack of a forty-pound badger cornered in its burrow. Packs of dachshunds were used to hunt wild boar, which are fierce and dangerous fighters. Today's dachshunds are the descendants of smaller, lighter versions used to hunt foxes and trail wounded deer.

Among the most ancient of the dog breeds are the polar group, found mainly in areas within the Arctic Circle. These are stocky dogs, very little changed from their wolf ancestors. They typically have erect ears, long pointed snouts framed by a ruff of fur, and up-curling tails; their heavy coats have the typical "wild" coloring. Dogs of the polar group are often referred to as *spitz* (which literally means "pointed"—from their characteristic muzzle shape). The Norwegian elkhound is a typical spitz-type dog, with an up-curling tail and plenty of northern wolf in its ancestry. In addition to hunting elk (large members of the deer family), these dogs have a six-thousand-year history that includes herding flocks, protecting people and livestock from bears and wolves, and adventuring in the longships with the Viking explorers.

It's a bit of a mystery how the Rhodesian Ridgeback wound up in the hound group. It was bred by the Boer farmers of South Africa from a mixture of Great Danes, mastiffs, greyhounds, terriers, bloodhounds, pointers, spaniels, and setters, together with the native African Hottentot dog. From this mixture the Boers produced the dog they needed: a loyal, affectionate animal that could withstand the freezing nights and burning days of the African bush, go twenty-four hours without water, hunt with the master, and guard his wife, children, and farm from predators and prowlers at night.

WORKING DOGS

In addition to the hunting breeds, dogs have been bred for a variety of jobs. The eighteen breeds currently registered in the AKC working dogs group are:

Akita	Komondor
Alaskan malamute	Kuvasz
Bernese mountain dog	Mastiff
Boxer	Newfoundland
Bullmastiff	Rottweiler
Doberman pinscher	Saint Bernard
Giant schnauzer	Samoyed
Great Dane	Siberian husky
Great Pyrenees	Standard schnauzer

The Akita is the only dog that has been declared a national monument. It was first bred in the early seventeenth century in the mountains of Japan, as a hunting dog and guard dog. The Akita's upstanding ears, large, sturdy body, thick coat, and up-curling tail show its spitz-type, northern wolf ancestry. At one time, only the imperial family and ruling aristocrats of Japan were allowed to own an Akita. By 1931, however, this dog breed had become so widely known and beloved that the Japanese government designated the Akita a national monument and national treasure. Even today the government will help pay for the care and feeding of an Akita champion if the owner cannot do so. Akitas now work mainly as guard dogs and baby-sitters; they are very affectionate with the family and friends but fierce in defending them against strangers. Akitas were brought to the United States by returning GIs after World War II. The Japanese regard the Akita as a loyal companion and a symbol of good health; a typical gift when a baby is born is a small statue of an Akita to symbolize health, happiness, and a long life. The statues are also sent as "get-well" presents when someone is ill. Dog-lovers all over Japan know the story of Hachiko, an Akita whose master was a professor at Tokyo University. Each day the dog accompanied his master to the railroad station to see him off on his commuting trip to work, and each evening Hachiko would be at the station again in time to welcome his master back. But one afternoon in 1925, Hachiko's master died at the university. The dog waited patiently until midnight, then finally went home. The next evening he was at the station again, waiting for his master who would never return. For the next nine years, Hachiko returned to the train station each night; he didn't miss a single night until he died. Today a statue of Hachiko, the faithful Akita, stands at the Shibuya railroad station in Tokyo to remind people of his loyalty.

The Alaskan malamute and Siberian husky are sled dogs of the Arctic region. These large dogs look very wolflike, except for their up-curling "spitz" tails.

The thick fur of these sled dogs protects them from the bitter cold.

Their thick fur coat helps to protect them against the bitter Arctic cold; it consists of a very soft, dense undercoat and an outer coat of coarser, longer guard hairs that are banded with colors to give an overall "gray wolf" look. Alaskan natives and visiting explorers harness the malamutes and huskies in teams to sledges that they pull along the snow and ice. The dogs are amazingly hardy. In 1958 a team of researchers who had taken huskies down to Antarctica had to leave two of their sled dogs behind when they left for the winter. When the scientists returned to the Antarctic station in the spring, the dogs were waiting to greet them. There have been reports that the Alaskan natives periodically breed malamutes and huskies back to wolves by leaving bitches in heat chained out where male wolves can get to them. In this way they keep the breed strong and vital. The

Alaskan malamutes and Siberian huskies registered with the AKC are purebred dogs with long pedigrees, but in their native Arctic the term husky is also used for a variety of mixed-breed sled dogs.

The Samoyed, the oldest member of the northern spitz group, has a pure white coat. These beautiful dogs are hard workers, guarding reindeer and pulling sledges in the northern parts of the USSR. Samoyeds have been taken as sled dogs on a number of Arctic and Antarctic expeditions. They are extremely intelligent dogs, gentle and loyal to humans, with a cheerful disposition.

When chance mutations produced giant dogs, ancient breeders were quick to capitalize on the lucky accident. The mutants were treasured and carefully bred and soon became valuable trade items. The ancestors of the mastiffs are thought to have arisen in northern India. By around 1000 B.C. they were popping up in carvings on Egyptian monuments and on sculpture in Assyria. Chinese literature refers to them as early as 1121 B.C. The ancient Greeks bred mastiffs, and the Romans gave them their modern name, from the Latin word *mansuetus*, "tame," referring to their use as family guard dogs. Writing about his invasion of Britain in 55 B.C., Julius Caesar described huge dogs that fought courageously beside their British masters against the Roman legions. Some of these British mastiffs were brought back to Rome and matched against human gladiators, bulls, bears, lions,

During the Middle Ages, dogs were often outfitted in armor such as this, a style popular in Germany in the mid-1500s.

and tigers at the Circus Maximus. Through the Middle Ages, mastiffs continued to be used as fighting dogs in wars. They were often outfitted with coats of armor; sometimes they carried leather-mounted knives or flaming torches. Their job was to dash among the enemy's cavalry to frighten and disrupt the horses.

Although mastiffs were well known as fighting

dogs, they were also used as hunting dogs and especially as guard dogs. During Anglo-Saxon times in Britain, peasants were required by law to keep at least one mastiff for each two peasants. The dogs were sometimes called "tiedogs" because they were kept tied during the day and let loose at night; they helped to keep wolves and other wild animals under control.

A number of other breeds are descended from mastiff ancestors. In the nineteenth century, gamekeepers in England, trying to keep the estates they managed free of poachers, decided they needed better watchdogs. The mastiffs were huge and powerful but not fast enough. Bulldogs were strong and active, but they were not large enough and they were too ferocious. (The gamekeeper would not want to *kill* a poacher just for setting a snare for a rabbit.) So they crossed mastiffs and bulldogs and came up with the ideal guard dog, the bullmastiff. Bullmastiffs were trained to follow a trespasser, warn him with a growl, and if he paid no attention, to knock him down and keep him off his feet until humans came to arrest him. Being hit by 130 pounds of muscular dog was enough to discourage most poachers, but if an intruder put up a struggle or was armed, the dog would seize him by the arm and squeeze, harder and harder, until the bone was about to break. (These guard dogs were holders, not biters.) Today bullmastiffs make good watchdogs; they are gentle and affectionate, especially with children, and fiercely loyal to the owner's family.

In Germany, mastiffs brought by Roman legions were bred into the Rottweiler, which was used as a combination drover (herding dog) and bank guard. Farmers driving their cattle to market had Rottweilers to help manage the herd; then after the cattle were sold, they didn't have to worry about having their money stolen by highwaymen on the way home. They just fastened it in leather bags to the dogs' collars.

Another German mastiff breed is the boxer. This sturdy, square-built dog also has a little terrier in its ancestry. It was originally bred for fighting, before dogfighting and bullbaiting were outlawed. Its curious fighting style gave the boxer its name: it starts a fight with its front paws, using them somewhat like a man boxing. Today the boxer's role is that of guard dog or police dog. Alert and courageous while guarding, this powerful dog can be playful with its owner's family and friends and is very patient with children.

Mastiffs were the ancestors of a number of large dogs used to guard flocks of sheep and goats in various parts of Europe. These include the Great Pyrenees of the mountainous Basque regions between France and Spain and the komondor and Kuvasz of Hungary. Basque fishermen took mastiff-type dogs to Canada, and these were the ancestors of the black Newfoundland dogs used for sea rescue work. Mastiff-type Bernese mountain dogs worked as drovers, draft animals, and watchdogs in Berne, Switzerland. In the Swiss mountains, mastiff stock gave rise to the

This young Saint Bernard belongs to the famous Hospice in Switzerland.

huge Saint Bernard. Bred from mastiffs brought by the Roman legions and native dogs present at the time, Saint Bernards worked at first as guard dogs, herders, and draft animals. During the seventeenth century, these dogs began to serve as watchdogs and companions for the monks who ran the hospice at the Saint Bernard pass, a refuge for travelers crossing the mountains between Switzerland and Italy. The monks found that the Saint Bernards, with their keen sense of smell and acute heat sense, were able to locate travelers lost in swirling snowstorms. They also have an uncanny ability to sense an approaching avalanche.

Mastiffs were the ancestors of another giant of the dog world, the Great Dane. Our name for this dog comes from the French, who called it the "grand Danois." No one knows why the French used this name, nor why English-speaking peoples adopted it instead of one of half a dozen other names current in France. Actually, the Great Dane's history has nothing to do with Denmark; it was bred in Germany about four hundred years ago as a hound for hunting wild boars. A huge, strong, swift dog was needed to tackle the savage and powerful boar, and that is what the breeders got. Great Dane fanciers call it the "king of dogs." German Great Dane breeders have been trying since 1880 to get the world to call their creation the "Deutsche dogge," but no one seems to be paying much attention to their plea.

The Doberman pinscher was the creation of one

Even sitting still, the Doberman pinscher does not look like an animal you'd want to cross.
Courtesy the American Kennel Club.

man, a German tax collector named Ludwig Dober-mann, who set out to breed the ideal guard and police dog in the late 1800s. Local shepherd dogs, Rottweiler, black-and-tan terrier, and smooth-haired German pinscher all went into the mix. What developed was a large, deceptively sleek but powerful dog, highly intelligent, rather nervous, with a keen nose and a strong sense of territory. The Doberman's lop ears are usually cropped to stand up straight, and its tail is docked (cut short); both these changes are designed to help it in its work, providing less for a criminal to grab hold of when the dog is helping its handler make an arrest. They also make the dog look more aggressive. The Doberman's keen intelligence and nervous temperament call for a skilled and forceful handler, and indeed, this breed has long had a reputation for viciousness. Recently, however, breeders have made the Doberman a more manageable dog, still fiercely effective in attack and defense but more suitable as a family watchdog.

Few people realize that the giant schnauzer, the standard schnauzer, and the miniature schnauzer (which is listed in the toy group) are not merely size variations of a single breed. Instead, they are actually three distinct breeds of dog that were developed separately and eventually reached a rather similar appearance. The standard schnauzer is the oldest of these three German breeds; one was depicted in paintings by Albrecht Dürer back in 1492. It is a compact, square-built dog with a typical schnauzer face sporting bushy eyebrows and whiskers, and it was apparently bred from a mixture of poodle, spitz, and wirehaired pinscher. Standard schnauzers were originally used as rat catchers, yard dogs, and guards. The giant schnauzers were first bred for herding sheep and driving cattle. Both breeds are used in Germany as police dogs, but in the United States and England the standard schnauzer is mainly a guard dog or a companion.

HERDING DOGS

In 1982 the American Kennel Club decided that the working dog group, with more than thirty breeds, was getting unwieldy. Eighteen breeds were left in the original working group, and fourteen breeds were placed in a separate group of herding dogs:

Australian cattle dog	Collie
Bearded collie	German Shepherd dog
Belgian Malinois	Old English sheepdog
Belgian sheepdog	Puli
Belgian Tervuren	Shetland sheepdog
Bouvier des Flandres	Welsh corgi, Cardigan
Briard	Welsh corgi, Pembroke

Like the working dogs, the members of the herding group are all still able to do the jobs for which they were bred: in this case, herding sheep or driving cattle. Even in show dogs, which have been bred mainly for appearance, the old instincts are still active.

The Belgian Malinois, Belgian sheepdog (sometimes called the Groenendael), and the Belgian Tervuren are actually the same dog, wearing different coats. Until 1891 the Belgian sheepdog was a mixed category including shepherd dogs of varying sizes, shapes, and colors, found throughout most of Europe. Then a study of the various types was made, and it was discovered that three kinds resembled one another rather closely, except that one had a long black coat, one was a shorthaired fawn and charcoal, and one was shaggy-haired with a dark ash-gray coat. The Belgian Kennel Club decided to accept only these three types for dog shows and encouraged breeders to breed only dogs of the same coat type together. Today the Malinois is the shorthaired fawn and black dog, the Groenendael is longhaired and black, and the Tervuren has a long, shaggy coat of reddish fawn in which each hair is tipped with black; its underparts, tail, and "breeches" are light beige.

A popular sheepdog is the collie, a breed developed in Scotland. The collie is thought to be a very ancient dog, but exactly how old is not known—the Scottish dog breeders were not in the habit of keeping records. There are two collie varieties: rough, with long, shaggy hair; and smooth, with short hair. (The famous fictional dog Lassie was a rough collie.) Both varieties get their slim, pointed muzzle and long, light-boned body from gazehound ancestors; northern spitz-type ancestors contributed hardiness in cold weather. The popularity of collies dates back to Queen Victoria of England, who saw them for the first time when she visited Balmoral, Scotland, fell in love with the breed, and sponsored them enthusiastically. These days there is not much call for working shepherd dogs, but collies have found a new place as companion dogs. They are devoted family pets, affectionate with children, and they consistently rank in the top ten pet breeds.

The Shetland sheepdog looks like a miniature of the rough collie, but it is actually a separate breed, developed to suit the rough terrain of its home. (It comes from the same region of Scotland as the Shetland pony.) The Border collie is a fine sheepdog and

This Border collie crouches low and stares at the sheep in order to get them to retreat into a pen. This instinctive behavior by the dog along with the instinct of the sheep to flock together help get the sheep penned without too much running, which is not good for them.

Courtesy Lorna Coppinger, Hampshire College, Amherst, Massachusetts.

companion. It is recognized as a breed by the Kennel Club of Great Britain, but the American Kennel Club places it in the "miscellaneous" class, candidates for registration in the future. The bearded collie is another Scottish shepherd breed, which appeared in portraits of British nobles back in the late 1700s.

The Old English sheepdog has a large head, a square-built sturdy body, and long hair that covers its body and legs and falls over its eyes. Its name is rather misleading. It is an English dog, although its ancestry is rather uncertain (claims are made for the Scottish bearded collie and the Russian Owtchar). But it is not as old as other sheepdog breeds, and it has actually been used more as a drover's dog, for driving sheep and cattle to market, than as a shepherd. The practice of docking the tails of Old English sheepdog puppies when they are three to four days old dates back to an old law stating that drovers' dogs were exempt from taxes; a docked tail was the dog's proof of its occupation. Today these sheepdogs make good companions that are at home in any climate: their long coats serve as insulation against heat, cold, and dampness.

The Bouvier des Flandres is a powerfully built, rough-coated dog that worked originally as a cattle driver and general farm dog. The breed was almost wiped out during World War I, when areas of Belgium where the dogs were bred were devastated. A few dedicated breeders managed to bring their dogs safely through the war. Today Bouvier fanciers are trying to preserve the dog's original qualities as a working dog. In Belgium no Bouvier can win the title of champion unless it has also won a prize in a work competition as a police, defense, or army dog. Bouviers have been used as messenger dogs, watchdogs, and guide dogs for the blind.

The briard is a very old breed of French working dogs; pictures of it appear in tapestries dating back to the eighth century. Briards have a very strong herding instinct, and if no sheep are in their charge they will try to herd anything available, nudging their master to keep him on the track and preventing his children from straying beyond the boundaries of the family property. They are extremely anxious to please; when they were used as war dogs, carrying supplies and leading medical corpsmen to the wounded on the battlefield, they tended to work themselves to exhaustion. But a briard can be independent-minded, too, viewing itself as a family companion rather than a servant—not a dog for people who expect instant obedience.

The puli, a dark-colored drover dog that comes from Hungary, has an unusual coat. Its undercoat is soft, dense, and very wooly, and its outer coat is long and thick. As the puli grows, its undercoat tangles with its outer coat to form long cords of matted hair that help to protect it in its work. The dark color was bred to make the puli easier to see during the daytime as it worked around the light-colored sheep. (Other

Hungarian sheepdogs, the light-colored komondor and Kuvasz, specialized in protecting the flocks from robbers and predators at night.)

The Pembroke Welsh corgi and the Cardigan Welsh corgi are actually two different breeds of cattle dogs. The Cardigan (which has a tail) was brought to Wales by Celts from Central Europe around 1200 B.C. The Pembroke (which is tailless) was brought by Flemish weavers invited to Wales by King Henry I in 1107 A.D. The name corgi comes from words meaning "dwarf dog." Both corgis are short-legged dogs of northern wolf ancestry. The corgi's original jobs were to flush out game and to guard its owner's children. Later, when most of the land in Wales was owned by the crown but tenant farmers were permitted to graze their cattle on open land, there was a great deal of competition for grazing space. The clever farmers used their corgis to nip at the heels of their neighbors' cattle and scatter them, leaving the land free for their own herds. The corgis' short legs permitted them to dash in and out safely between the legs of the cattle.

The German Shepherd was originally bred as a herding sheepdog, but now it is far more commonly used as a watchdog, guide dog, and police dog. (In fact, *Webster's New Collegiate Dictionary* lists "German Shepherd" as the second meaning for "police dog.") One of the most popular breeds in America today, the German Shepherd looks rather wolflike. It is highly intelligent, loyal, and courageous, with an

German Shepherds are used in New York City to help patrol the subways.

even disposition and well-controlled nerves. It works well with people, and whether guarding or guiding it can use judgment, rather than leaping off on hair-trigger reflexes.

TERRIERS

Terrier comes from the Latin word *terra*, meaning "earth." The small, compact dogs in the terrier group were able to go to earth, digging into tunnels and diving down holes after their prey. The AKC currently recognizes twenty-three breeds of terriers:

Airedale terrier	Lakeland terrier
American Staffordshire terrier	Manchester terrier
	Miniature schnauzer
Australian terrier	Norfolk terrier
Bedlington terrier	Norwich terrier
Border terrier	Scottish terrier
Bull terrier	Sealyham terrier
Cairn terrier	Skye terrier
Dandie Dinmont terrier	Soft-coated wheaten terrier
Fox terrier	Staffordshire bull terrier
Irish terrier	Welsh terrier
Kerry blue terrier	West Highland white terrier

Terriers are scrappy little dogs, with courage out of all proportion to their size. They were bred to chase, attack, and kill the vermin that plagues farmers: rats, rabbits, weasels, and foxes. Absolutely fearless, they will attack animals many times their size, and they are such ferocious fighters that terriers were used in dog-fighting and animal baiting. And yet terriers can also be playful, the clowns of the dog world.

The largest of the terriers is the Airedale, a wiry-haired English terrier bred from the old black-and-tan terrier (a breed that no longer exists) and the otter hound. The Airedale is an enthusiastic hunter that has even been used to capture lions and bears. It can also work as a shepherd dog, protecting the flock from predators, and it can be used as a retriever. Airedales were among the first breeds selected for police work in

Germany and England, and they have been used in wars as dispatch bearers, loyally delivering their dispatches even after being wounded. Though they are fierce fighters, Airedales have a sweet disposition with the humans they love.

The Bedlington is a graceful long-legged dog with a shape that reveals some whippet mixed with its terrier ancestors. (Like the whippet, this terrier will race swiftly after a rabbit.) It has a crisp, slightly curly coat. Like other terriers, the Bedlington was bred for killing rats and other vermin. In the early and mid-1800s, miners in the Bedlington region of England matched their terriers in fights to the death, cheering their favorites and betting on the outcome. When dogfighting was outlawed, Bedlingtons became favored pets among the upper class, especially the ladies, who prized their elegant appearance and gentle and lovable disposition.

The bull terrier was bred specially for dogfighting, from a cross of bulldog and terrier. The result was a strong, agile, courageous dog. Although we now consider the sport of dogfighting cruel, the men who trained the dogs and bet on the fights had a highly developed sense of fair play. Their dogs were taught to defend themselves courageously but not to seek or provoke a fight. A white variety of the bull terrier was nicknamed "the white cavalier." Other dogs bred for fighting were the American Staffordshire terrier and the Staffordshire bull terrier, as well as the pit bull

Courtesy Evelyn M. Shafer.
The curly-coated Bedlington terrier has a distinctive cone-top head.

terrier, which is not recognized as a breed by the AKC. It is a pity these dogs gained a reputation as vicious fighters; actually they are friendly, playful and affectionate dogs that make good companions.

The Dandie Dinmont terrier was named after a fictional character in a novel by Sir Walter Scott, *Guy Mannering,* published in 1814. The fictional Dandie Dinmont was a farmer who had six dogs: Auld Pepper, Auld Mustard, Young Pepper, Young Mustard, Little Pepper, and Little Mustard. The terrier breed that was given his name actually existed long before the book was written. It is a small, muscular dog with a large head and thick, two-inch-long hair. Originally bred to hunt otters and badgers, it is now mainly a house dog.

Fox terriers were bred to run with the hounds. If

Courtesy Evelyn M. Shafer.
The Dandie Dinmont terrier does, indeed, look like a dandy.

the fox took refuge in a burrow or drainpipe, it was the fox terrier's job to go in after it and flush it out. Two varieties, smooth and wirehaired, originally were not kept separate, and puppies with smooth coats and wiry coats often occurred in the same litter. Fox terriers are lively and active and are among the best known and most widely owned of purebred dogs.

While the English upper class engaged in fox hunts, people of the working class enjoyed cheaper sports. Dogs such as the Manchester terrier were bred for the sport of ratting. Ferrets were sent down rodent holes and drove the inhabitants of the burrows up to the surface. There the terriers waited to pounce on the rodents and kill them before they could run to another hole. The slim black and tan Manchester terrier was a skillful rat killer. (But the champion ratter of all time was a bull terrier bitch named Jenny Lind, who killed five hundred rats in just an hour and a half.) A whippet ancestor also gave the Manchester terrier the speed it needed for coursing rabbits. Today this small terrier with clean habits makes an intelligent house pet and companion.

The Scottish terrier, or "Scottie," is the best known of a variety of small longhaired terriers from Scotland which date back to the fourteenth century. A great deal of breeding has taken place since then, however. Though today's Scottish terrier is a sturdy little animal, it probably could not hunt foxes in the rocky terrain of Scotland, as its ancestors did.

The miniature schnauzer is the third member of the schnauzer trio. (We met the other two in the working dogs group.) Although it resembles the various terriers bred in England to go to ground after vermin, the miniature schnauzer was bred in Germany from affenpinschers, poodles, and small standard schnauzers. It has a happy temperament and makes a good pet, devoted to its home and family and able to bark an alarm just as well as any regular-sized guard dog. The miniature schnauzer has become a sort of status symbol, prized as an elegant pet, commanding huge prices, and generally owned by people who can afford to buy it frills like diamond-studded collars.

TOYS

Toys may not be classed as working dogs, but they have a job to do: to keep people happy. There are seventeen breeds in the group:

Affenpinscher
Brussels griffon
Chihuahua
English toy spaniel
Italian greyhound
Japanese Chin
Maltese
Manchester terrier (toy)
Miniature pinscher
Papillon
Pekingese
Pomeranian
Poodle (toy)
Pug
Shih Tzu
Silky terrier
Yorkshire terrier

The toys are generally midgets or dwarfs of larger breeds. (Midgets are tiny, well-proportioned miniatures of the ancestral breed; dwarfs are stocky, short-legged dogs with flattened faces.) The ancestry of the toy poodle, the toy Manchester terrier, the English toy spaniel, and the Italian greyhound is obvious. The miniature pinscher is not a smaller version bred from the Doberman pinscher, however; its breed is actually several hundred years older than the Doberman. The affenpinscher, a dog with a comical monkey-like face, is closely related to it and, in turn, was one of the ancestors of the Brussels griffon. The papillon (*papillon* is the French word for "butterfly") has large, expressive ears; it is a midget spaniel. (In the sixteenth century, lop-eared versions of the papillon were known as the dwarf spaniel, but with its well-proportioned body and fine-boned, slender legs, the papillon is a scaled-down miniature—a midget rather than a dwarf.) The Pomeranian is a spitz-type midget, a miniature version of the sturdy Arctic sled dogs. The pug, which looks like a miniature bulldog, comes from dwarfed mastiff stock. The Yorkshire terrier, a tiny longhaired terrier, was bred down from the Skye terrier in just twenty years. The Yorkie, in turn, was crossed with the Australian terrier to produce the silky terrier.

Many of the toy breeds were at first kept only by

These Yorkshire terrier pups make it easy to see why many people find toys irresistible.

Courtesy Ruth F. Almstedt.

rich nobles. (The Yorkshire terrier is an exception. It was bred originally as a dog of the working classes but later became a favorite pet of rich Victorian ladies.) A large proportion of the toys originated in the Far East, especially in China, where for thousands of years there was a powerful ruling class with enough time and money to indulge in luxuries.

The Pekingese is a longhaired dwarf dog of China. It is a very ancient dog; the earliest record of it dates back to the eighth century. The Pekingese was considered sacred in ancient China. Its bloodlines were kept very pure, and only the imperial family was permitted to own this breed. (Anyone caught stealing one of the sacred dogs was put to death.) The Pekingese was not introduced into the Western world until 1860, when British soldiers won a battle in Peking and looted the Imperial Palace. Four little Pekingese owned by the aunt of the Chinese emperor were found hiding behind a drapery and were taken back to England. One was presented to Queen Victoria; British nobles kept the other three and bred them.

The Japanese Chin originated in China and was introduced into Japan when a Chinese emperor presented a pair to the emperor of Japan. Although these dogs were kept only by nobles, the Japanese had no restrictions against sharing them with the rest of the world. In fact, Japanese Chin were often given as gifts to visiting diplomats and foreigners who had rendered some outstanding service. This is a dainty little dog with the typical shortened muzzle of a dwarf but the slim, small-boned legs of a midget.

The English toy spaniel, despite its name, was another import from the Far East; it originated in Japan and China. It appears to have reached England some time in the sixteenth century.

The pug is another toy breed that originated in China (more than two thousand years ago) and eventually was carried to Europe. In Holland the pug became the official dog of the ruling House of Orange after one of this breed barked an alarm at the approach of Spanish invaders in 1572 and saved the life of William, Prince of Orange. In France this miniature dog became popular among the nobles. The Empress Josephine had a pug named Fortune who was a pugnacious little dog. When Napoleon entered his wife's bedroom on their wedding night, the pug bit him. Perhaps he was jealous.

Shih Tzu means "lion dog." It looks rather like a lion as depicted in Oriental art, although to Western eyes this longhaired toy looks more like an animated floor mop. Paintings and documents from 624 A.D. indicate that a pair of Shih Tzu was brought to the Chinese court from the Byzantine empire. Other legends suggest that the dog originated in Tibet. The breed was a favorite of the Chinese royal family, and certain members of the court competed to breed varieties of the dog that would take the emperor's fancy. When the emperor walked about, he was preceded by Shih Tzu pets who barked to warn lesser mortals not to gaze upon their divine ruler.

The origin of the Chihuahua is a mystery. Stone carvings show that it was raised mainly as food by the Toltecs of Mexico in the eighth or ninth century, and that a similar dog was living in Central America at the time. Yet this little dog is clearly related to the dogs of the Middle East. Presumably companion dogs were carried somehow from Asia to the New World—perhaps on ships across the Atlantic, on reed boats across the Pacific, or even overland by way of the land bridge that used to exist between Siberia and Alaska. Present-day Chihuahuas are bred in two varieties, long coat and smooth coat.

Toy dogs were bred to be just the right size to sit on a lap (or in the Far East, to be carried in a sleeve). Because they look so cute, people tend to think of them as animated toys. But these miniatures are all dog—intelligent, alert, and scrappy, ready to challenge the world. Roger Caras tells of a papillon that used to take on bloodhounds thirty times his weight and send them away yelping; he had the mailman so terrorized that he refused to deliver mail to the house even after the dog was gone. (The papillon fell madly in love with a visiting Yorkshire terrier and pined away so badly after she left that he was sent to live with her owner.) Even a Chihuahua, the tiniest of all dogs, can make a good watchdog, defending its territory and barking an alarm at intruders.

NON-SPORTING DOGS

This is a sort of catchall group, for dogs that don't seem obviously to fit into any of the other groups. The non-sporting dogs currently include eleven breeds:

Bichon frise
Boston terrier
Bulldog
Chow chow
Dalmatian
French bulldog

Keeshond
Lhasa Apso
Poodle
Schipperke
Tibetan terrier

The chow chow is a very ancient dog, bred in China at least two thousand years ago. It is a sturdy, powerful dog with a thick fluffy coat and a furry ruff around its head. The red-gold variety looks rather like a lion, and in ancient China chows served as temple guards. (Their memory survives today in the statues of "lion-dogs," or stylized chows, at the gates of Chinese temples.) The chow chow's up-curling tail and heavy build put it in the spitz group; it is thought to be the result of a cross of a mastiff from Tibet and the Samoyed from Siberia. The chow chow is the only dog breed that possesses a blue-black tongue. Today chows are pets and guard dogs, but in China they were the main sporting dog and were also raised as a source of food. (Chinese cuisine includes a great variety of recipes for dog, which is still regarded as a delicacy there.) The name "chow chow" apparently came from the pidgin English term for knickknacks or bric-a-brac. Instead of detailing all the items in their cargo, sea captains returning from the Orient simply logged in "chow chow" to indicate miscellaneous goods. Since Chinese dogs were often included in the cargo, the term came to be applied to them, too.

From the early thirteenth century until it was outlawed in 1835, bullbaiting was a popular sport in England. Several dogs were set loose on a bull in a ring or in a village square, while musicians played, refreshments were served, and people watched the sport. The attacks of the dogs enraged the bull, who tried to shake them loose and gore them. The bulldog was bred for this sport from mastiff and terrier stock. Its job was to attack viciously and hold on tenaciously. After bullbaiting and dogfighting were outlawed, bulldog fanciers preserved the breed as a companion and guard dog. They kept its broad, heavy body and typical bulldog face, but they bred out the viciousness. Today's bulldog is a mild-mannered, affectionate companion, but it is still physically tough with a built-in instinct for holding on tight, no matter what. Zoologist John McLoughlin tells of watching his father play with his pet English bulldogs. Gripping one end of a length of rubber garden hose while the dog held on to the other with its powerful jaws, he would swing the heavy dog around and around in the air. Finally he would tire and let go of the hose, and the dog would go sailing out over the lawn. As soon as

Courtesy Mary Bloom.
Despite his fierce expression and thick, "fighter" build, the bulldog is an affectionate companion.

it landed, it would bound back, carrying the hose, for more fun.

The French bulldog is a smaller variation, apparently descended from toy bulldogs sent over from England in the late nineteenth century. The Boston terrier was bred in America from a cross of an English bulldog and a white English terrier. A dog named Judge, imported to Boston in 1870, was the ancestor of nearly all the Boston terriers alive today.

The Dalmatian, with its distinctive coat of white with small black spots, is a very old breed that has come through many centuries unchanged. It gets its name from Dalmatia, a province of Austria, which was its first home as far as we know. But some people believe that the spotted dog depicted following a chariot in an ancient Egyptian engraving was a Dalmatian, too. At various times the Dalmatian has been used as a shepherd, a hunting dog, a draft dog, an army sentinel, and a guard dog. Its excellent memory has made it a star of circuses and stage shows. But the Dalmatian's real talent is for following wheeled vehicles. Through the centuries it accompanied chariots, coaches, and finally fire engines. (The Dalmatian is the firehouse mascot.) The Dalmatian's chasing behavior is a built-in instinct. In fact, different strains

Dalmatians are perhaps best known as firehouse mascots.
Courtesy Evelyn M. Shafer.

run below the axles of carriages, in front of carriages, or behind carriages; there are also strains that ride on carriages. The behavior of each type is strictly hereditary. When a Dalmatian is kept as a pet, it may develop the dangerous habit of chasing cars.

The poodle is the number one pet dog in America and has been extremely popular in other countries as well—in so many places, in fact, that no one is quite sure where it originated. The Germans claim it and gave the dog its name, from *pudel* or *pudelin*, which means "to splash in water." (The poodle was originally used as a retriever, and unclipped it looks very much like English and Irish water spaniels.) The French regard the poodle as their national dog and have used it as a retriever and a traveling-circus dog. The practice of clipping off part of the poodle's coat was intended to make it easier for it to swim in its retrieving duties, but the French developed poodle clipping to an art. Poodles come in three sizes: standard (the oldest breed), miniature, and toy. Their coat may be black, white, or a variety of solid colors, and even the skin of the poodle varies from pink or blue to silver or cream. Poodle fanciers can pick a pet to match their decor! The poodle is not merely decorative, however; it is an extremely intelligent animal.

The Lhasa Apso looks like a decorative lapdog, but in its native Tibet it is called the "bark lion sentinel dog." In the Tibetan lamaseries, a huge mastiff is kept chained at the outer door, while the Lhasa Apso serves as a guard inside. It is an intelligent little animal, with keen hearing, able to quickly distinguish friends from strangers. Another Tibetan dog, the Tibetan terrier, is raised as a pet and is thought to bring the family good luck. No Tibetan would ever sell a Tibetan terrier, because that would be selling part of their luck, but they will give a dog away in gratitude for favors or services. Why the dog is called a Tibetan terrier is a mystery, since it is not related to the terriers and looks like an old English sheepdog. The long hair of the Tibetan dogs provides insulation against the cold of the high mountains.

The 1983 Christmas catalog from the exclusive retailing firm Neiman-Marcus featured a "Rare gift: His and Hers": Shar-Pei puppies for $2,000 each. The Shar-Pei is not a new breed—it has been traced back as far as the Han dynasty in China, from 206 B.C. to 220 A.D. Originally bred as a fighting dog, the Shar-Pei seems to have enough skin for two dogs; its flesh hangs in baggy folds all over its head and body. This loose skin is a defense mechanism: if the dog is seized by an opponent, it can turn all the way around inside its own skin and bite back. The Shar-Pei nearly became extinct. In the 1950s there were only twelve of these dogs left in all the world. Then a Shar-Pei named Jones Faigoo was brought to the United States in 1966, and interest in the unusual dog grew rapidly. The Shar-Pei was still listed in the *Guiness Book of World Records* as the world's rarest dog breed as late

Courtesy Claudia Chapman.
The baggy-skinned Shar-Pei is making a comeback from near extinction.

as 1979, but by 1983 there were 2,495 registered with the Chinese Shar-Pei Club of America. Owners are finding that despite their fighting past, today's Shar-Pei are gentle, friendly dogs, extremely clean (they usually housebreak themselves within a month), and intelligent.

PUREBRED OR OVERBRED?

Many people who are concerned about animals are becoming troubled about some dog breeding practices and the problems that are cropping up among purebred dogs. Some of the characteristics that dog fanciers prize are actually deformities. Humans suffering from giantism or dwarfism, for example, are viewed as unfortunate victims of endocrine disorders, and medical researchers are actively seeking new and better ways to treat them. And yet, giant dogs such as Great Danes and Saint Bernards and dwarfs such as the Pekingese and Scottish terrier are carefully bred to keep their abnormal traits pure, and they command premium prices from buyers. Even among the dogs without major abnormalities, breeders sometimes concentrate on superficial appearance without giving much thought to the effects their breeding practices are having on the dog as a whole. Inbreeding can make hereditary problems even worse: often breeds were developed from a small number of original ancestors, and current champions are eagerly sought as sires, so that their genes are passed on widely. If only a small pool of dogs contributes to the heredity of a breed, any "bad genes" they may be carrying can be greatly magnified in later generations.

A 1981 report by the British Veterinary Association and the Kennel Club of England pointed out that this is exactly what is happening to many purebred dogs today. Giant dogs such as Saint Bernards, Great Danes, Great Pyrenees, British mastiffs, Newfoundlands, Irish wolfhounds, and Scottish deerhounds have much shorter life spans than smaller breeds and rarely live as long as ten years. They suffer from intestinal obstructions because there is not enough support for the sheer weight of their guts; they are also prone to heart attacks, hind leg and back problems, and chewing problems due to their abnormally shaped jaws. Dwarfs of the dog world are no better off: the Pekingese have breathing problems due to their short nose; they cannot chew normal foods because their teeth are not completely rooted in their stunted jaws; and their eyeballs protrude so much that they may dry out, may become ulcerated from the rubbing of skin folds on them, and are vulnerable to injury. The dachshund's long back makes it susceptible to back injuries and slipped disks. Basset hounds, too, suffer from back problems and slipped disks, as well as arthritis in their bent legs and distorted feet, eye problems including glaucoma, and infections in their long, floppy ears. Boxers and bulldogs suffer from respiratory and dental problems due to the shortness of nose and jaw; in addition, boxers are more likely than usual to die of cancer, and bulldogs suffer from a whole catalog of additional ailments including skin infections from bacteria trapped in the folds of skin and difficulties in giving birth. German Shepherds and cocker spaniels may suffer from epilepsy, and some breeds of terriers suffer from metabolic diseases. Dalmatians may suffer from gout and bladder stones.

Breeders are trying to correct some of these hereditary problems. A form of progressive blindness that occurs in Border collies has become much rarer since dogs entered in British sheepdog trials have been required to have an eye examination and only those free of the problem are entered in the stud book. But there has been much less success with a hereditary hip condition that afflicts some German Shepherds and Labradors and can lead to crippling arthritis.

In addition to their hereditary problems, some purebred dogs are subject to "cosmetic" operations such as ear cropping and tail docking. Concerned veterinarians continue to fight a losing battle against such practices, which they view as unnecessary mutilation.

The boxer's short nose and jaw give it frequent respiratory and dental problems.
Courtesy A.S.P.C.A.

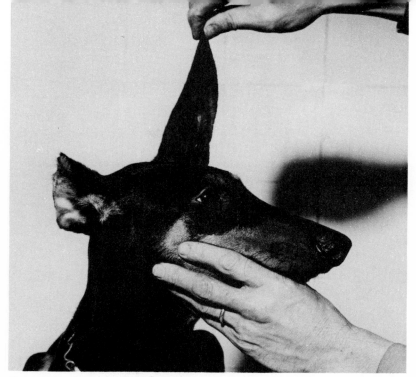

Courtesy Warren W. McSpadden for the A.S.P.C.A.
One of the breeding practices that concerns many veterinarians is ear cropping.

British veterinary surgeon Simon Wolfensohn points out that the current pedigree system concentrates on appearance and does not pay enough attention to the dog's general health. Dog breeding was originally a hobby, but now it has become a business. With pedigreed pups selling for hundreds of dollars, breeders try to produce animals that will win at dog shows and thus command top prices. This means sticking strictly to the breed standards and overusing champion breeding stocks. "Clearly," says Wolfensohn, "until the system is changed by modifying the breed standards when necessary, the situation will not improve."

Dogs as Pets

Dogs are the most popular of all pet animals, with cats in second place. More than half the households in America have dogs, and our pet dog population currently stands at nearly fifty million. We Americans take our pets seriously: in 1982 sales of children's toys in the United States totaled $222 million, but sales of pet accessories in that year came to more than $1.32 *billion*! That does not even count the nearly $5 billion spent on pet food.

Why do people keep pets? According to a recent survey, seventy-nine percent of pet owners keep animals for the pleasure of having them, thirty-three percent for protection, and eleven percent for rodent control. (That adds up to more than one hundred percent because some people have more than one reason for being pet owners.) The same survey indicated that most pet-owner relationships work out pretty well: eighty percent found their pets a source of cheerfulness, and seventy-three percent regarded them as a family member. On the other hand, seven percent considered their pets a nuisance, and four percent found them a financial burden.

According to the American Kennel Club, the most common registered dog breeds are poodles, cocker spaniels, Doberman pinschers, and Labrador retrievers. Those statistics don't count the purebred dogs that are not registered (including many German Shepherds, one of the most popular watchdogs) and the numerous mixed-breed mongrels. All of them are well equipped to provide the service that dogs do best: giving their owners loyalty, companionship, and unquestioning love.

CHOOSING A DOG

If you are planning to join the dog-owning majority, the first step is to decide what kind of dog you want. Of course, acquiring a dog often doesn't happen that way; instead, it's a case of love at first sight, a mysterious affinity springing up between a human and a bright-eyed ball of fur, and a yielding to an irresistible impulse. But if you do some thinking beforehand, you may be able to avoid some serious mistakes. Bringing home a dog means taking on a responsibility—one that you may have for ten or fifteen or even twenty years. It's not something that should be done lightly, on the spur of the moment.

Purebred or mutt? That's one question to consider. There are various arguments on each side, and the answers may add up differently for different people.

A purebred dog is more predictable. A full-grown dog may be quite different from that appealing puppy you've just fallen in love with. But at least if you know its breed, and perhaps even its family history, you will be able to predict fairly well how large it will grow, what it will look like as an adult and what kind of temperament it will have. With a mongrel you are taking potluck. It might turn out to be as bright, attractive, and charming as Benji of the movies; or it might manage to combine all the worst features of its varied ancestry. Roger Caras tells how he accidentally crossed a toy poodle with a pug. (He had thought the poodle was spayed.) The two "puggles" that resulted were the ugliest puppies he had ever seen, with a watermelon shape, a semi-corkscrew tail that would have looked appropriate on a pig, wispy black fur that curled in halfhearted corkscrews, a half-pushed-in face, and half-standing-up ears. He managed to find homes for both puppies, and they grew up to be ugly but lovable dogs, but it was not a combination he would ever want to repeat.

One problem with purebred dogs is that many breeds are highly inbred and prone to various health

Courtesy A.S.P.C.A.
The A.S.P.C.A. is a good source for loving, lovable companions.

problems; this is especially true of the giant and dwarf breeds. A mutt, on the other hand, is often hardier. Still another argument for mongrels—which for many people must be the deciding one—is that pure-bred dogs are often quite expensive, whereas mongrels can often be obtained free. (One of us had a yen for a

Pomeranian a few years ago but lost enthusiasm when we discovered they were selling for about $400 each.) Getting a dog from an animal shelter can give you a good feeling. Some shelters keep animals indefinitely, until they are placed for adoption, but most do not have enough space or money to do that; they keep animals only for a limited time and then put them painlessly to death if they have not been claimed. If you adopt one of these animals, you can feel that you are saving its life. Animal shelters usually charge a small fee, perhaps $5 to $15, and may also require a deposit to be returned after the animal has been neutered.

If you want a purebred dog, what breed would be best for you? Appearance is important—you want a dog you will enjoy looking at—but temperament can be even more important. Terriers, for example, are very lively, energetic dogs that suit some people perfectly, while others would be more comfortable with a dog with a calmer disposition. Sporting breeds and gazehounds are generally a poor choice if you live in an apartment in the city—unless, perhaps, you live near a park and have plenty of spare time to devote to exercising your dog. Small dogs are often the most practical for city dwellers, and the nonbarking basenji may be an ideal choice if you are worried about annoying the neighbors. But if you want your dog to act as a watchdog, then you want a dog that barks. (Watchdogs should be trained to warn, not to bite. An attack dog does not belong in a home with a family.) People with allergies may find that a curly-haired poodle or a smooth-coated Chihuahua will not cause them any problems. But the longhaired breeds should be avoided: pet allergies are usually provoked by the animals' hair and dander, the tiny flakes of dead skin from the base of the hairs. Another thing to think about if you are considering a longhaired dog is that they require daily grooming, which takes time and effort.

If you are choosing a mutt, you may be able to make some guesses about its adult appearance and temperament if you know what its parents were. Even then, they will only be guesses, since the workings of heredity are sometimes a bit chancy. (Playwright George Bernard Shaw was once approached by a beautiful woman who suggested that they should have a child, so that it could inherit her looks and his brains. "But Madam," he objected, "what if it has *my* looks and *your* brains?") The size of a puppy's paws can often give a rough idea of how large a dog it will be: the larger the paws, the larger the dog. (This rule doesn't always work, so if you pick out a tiny-pawed puppy that grows into a giant, don't blame us.)

Another question that should be resolved before you go dog-hunting is whether you want a puppy or an adult dog. Puppies are a lot of fun, and you don't have to worry about trying to break bad habits the dog has developed. But puppies can also be a great deal of trouble and work. They usually are not yet housebroken, are often noisy and boisterous, and they chew on everything. (Our eldest daughter came home from college one weekend when our dog, Jacqui, was about three months old. She ran some washer loads and decided to air-dry her favorite jeans. She draped them over the line on which Jacqui's chain slides and was promptly warned by her younger brother and sister that Jacqui would chew on them. "Oh, she wouldn't do that," our daughter scoffed—and got no sympathy when she complained a few hours later that the dog had chewed a hole in the leg of her best jeans.) An older dog is calmer and more settled and has already gone through the process of "socialization," learning to live with humans and obey various commands.

The best place to obtain a purebred dog is from a breeder who specializes in a particular breed or a few breeds and registers the animals with an organization like the American Kennel Club. You can obtain the address of a club representing the breed that interests you from the AKC. Copies of the club's magazine or newsletter will contain addresses of breeders. If there is no convenient breeder of the kind of dog you want, you can consider a pet shop. But check out the shop before you consider buying a dog, to make sure that it is clean and well ventilated, that the dogs are not kept confined in cages so small they can barely move around, and that they are fed regularly.

Some states have laws and regulations to protect

pet buyers. In our state of New Jersey, for example, each pet shop must display a sign advising you of your right to receive an Animal History Certificate, with information about the animal's breed, sex, age, birth date, breeder, the name of the veterinarian who examined it, and a statement of any vaccinations it has received. A dealer who says the animal is registered or can be registered must either register the animal or give you the necessary documents to do so within ninety days of the sale; otherwise you can return the animal for a full refund or keep it and receive a seventy-five percent refund. You also have fourteen days to return the animal if your veterinarian finds that it is ill or has some sort of birth defect. (Friends in Florida tell us that pet buyers there have only forty-eight hours to have a new pet examined for illness. You can check with your local Consumer Affairs department to find out what regulations protect you in your state.)

If you have decided that a mixed-breed is what you want, check with friends to see if anyone has a dog who has had or is expecting pups. Newspaper ads and supermarket bulletin boards often feature notices of "free puppies." Local animal shelters usually have a variety of puppies and dogs to choose from. In fact, if you are patient, you may even be able to get a purebred dog from an animal shelter—perhaps one whose owner has died or has moved to an apartment house that does not allow pets.

When choosing a dog, don't take one that is listless, bleary-eyed, runny-nosed, or has other obvious signs of illness, unless you are ready to cope with medical problems in addition to the normal adjustments. A puppy should be alert and curious, eager to explore its surroundings and to roughhouse with its littermates. Choose one that barks at you when you pass by, rather than one that backs away fearfully. A puppy that pays attention to you for ten to fifteen seconds is a better prospect than one that loses interest after only a few seconds. Check out its hearing by clapping your hands where it cannot see them and observe whether it reacts to the noise. Compare the puppy to its littermates: an obvious runt may grow into a fine dog if you give it extra care, but it may instead be an expensive headache that runs up veterinarian bills and cannot be trained satisfactorily. You are safer taking one of the larger pups in the litter.

A final word: Many parents yield to the temptation to get their children a dog for Christmas. A new puppy under the Christmas tree may seem like an appealing idea, but it is often much less appealing in reality. The bustle and excitement of unwrapping presents may frighten the puppy, and the children may have so many other gifts to distract them that they do not pay the dog enough attention. A better Christmas gift idea might be a picture of a dog or a little plastic or china miniature, together with an IOU. A few days later, when things have quieted down, the family can go to pick out the puppy together. Unless you live in a region that is warm all year round, it might be even better to forget about the idea of a Christmas puppy and wait until the spring or summer. Then you won't have to worry about bad weather when you want to take the puppy out for exercise.

HOME WITH A NEW DOG

You have found the dog you want—perhaps at a breeder's kennel, an animal shelter, or a pet shop—and it was love at first sight for both of you. Some money has changed hands, and you have received some instructions about feeding, puppy shots, and so forth. Now it's time to take the new dog home.

These days the trip home will probably involve traveling in a car or some other vehicle. If it's a car, at least two people should be along for the ride: one to drive and one to hold the dog. The driver needs to concentrate on the traffic and doesn't need an active puppy bounding into his or her lap and reaching up to give a friendly lick on the face—nor, for that matter, the distraction of a whining puppy if the new surroundings are frightening it. (Our Jacqui adored riding in cars from the very first, but she became restless whenever we stopped for a red light.) If you plan to use a bus or some other public transportation to take the dog home, you will need a sturdy carrier to keep it confined. You can't count on a new puppy's resting quietly in your arms for the whole trip; it might bolt suddenly and be lost or injured.

When you get home, the whole family will be excited about the new pet, but try to restrain some of the enthusiasm. The puppy has just been whisked away from its familiar surroundings, away from the comforting presence of its mother and littermates and all the people it knew. It needs some quiet time to get adjusted, to explore its new home and get acquainted with its new family at its own speed. If there are already other pets in the house, introduce them to the new dog under supervision, and try to give them their share of attention so that they will not be jealous. Be sure to have separate feeding bowls for the new puppy so that it will not be competing with the older pets for food.

The first night will be rough. During the day the

When a new pet arrives in your house, give it some quiet time to get adjusted to its surroundings.

Courtesy Alvin and Virginia Silverstein.

puppy had plenty of loving attention to distract it. You introduced it to its sleeping place when it was tired and wanted a nap; but when it woke up it could bound out and find some people to pet it and make a fuss over it. Now, however, the family is going to bed and you are going to be closing the door and leaving the puppy on its own. It will be alone for the first time in its whole life. Can you blame it for crying?

You can sympathize with the dog, but unless you don't mind having it sleep in your bed with you every night, be firm. It has its sleeping place: perhaps a basket-style or plastic dog bed (the plastic type, with washable covers for the cushion, is easy to keep clean) or a closed cardboard box with a hole cut in one side for a doorway and a nest of soft blankets or rags inside. You have your sleeping place. Don't make an exception and take it into bed with you "just this once." Dogs don't understand exceptions.

You can help ease the transition for a new puppy by placing a hot water bottle wrapped in a towel in its bed to substitute for the warmth of its mother and littermates. An old-fashioned wind-up clock with a loud tick, also wrapped in a towel, will remind the puppy of the sound of its mother's heartbeat and help to make it feel at home. Leaving a radio playing softly in the room and leaving a small light on can give it a feeling of company. Even so, it will probably bark and whine. Grit your teeth and try to ignore it. You may have another rough night or two to get through, but eventually the puppy will learn to accept its fate.

If you live in an apartment and have neighbors who might be bothered by the puppy's complaints, it is a good idea to speak to them beforehand, explain the situation, and assure them that the puppy will be sleeping quietly within a few days. This is also a good plan when you are training a dog to sleep in a kennel outdoors for the first time, or trying to accustom it to being chained or confined in a fenced-in run. Some fussing is to be expected: as far as the dog is concerned, you are depriving it of privileges that it regarded as its rights. But don't let your dog get into the habit of barking steadily for minutes on end, or holding loud long-distance conversations with other dogs in the neighborhood. You can't expect your neighbors to put up with that kind of nuisance indefinitely.

As soon as possible after you bring a new puppy or dog home, make an appointment with a veterinarian for a checkup. In addition to examining it for illnesses, birth defects, and worms, the vet will set up a schedule for injections to vaccinate the puppy against serious infectious diseases such as canine distemper, hepatitis, leptospirosis, and rabies.

A young puppy needs to eat frequently: up to the age of three months or so it is growing extremely rapidly and will need three or even four meals a day. After that, when the puppy's stomach is large enough to handle more food at a time, you can gradually give it more food in a smaller number of meals, cutting down to two meals a day after six months and perhaps even to a single feeding a day after one year.

Even an eight-week-old puppy, just brought home, is ready for some training. You can start on getting it housebroken, begin getting it accustomed to wearing a collar, and start teaching it some simple commands. One warning note: check the collar frequently! It's hard to believe how fast a puppy grows, and you probably won't notice the difference because it happens a little at a time and you see your puppy every day. But a collar that fit comfortably one week (loose enough so that you can slip a finger underneath but not so loose that the puppy can slip its head out) may be choking it the next week.

TRAINING

In training your dog, you have one important thing going for you: your dog really, sincerely wants to please you. It can't help it—that is built into a dog's genes. Why, then, are there so many problem dogs? (The title of one popular book on dog training is *Help! This Animal Is Driving Me Crazy!*) The answer is that although the dog wants to please you, sometimes it has trouble figuring out what you want it to do. Since you are smarter than a dog, it is your job to break through the communication gap and make it understand.

There are many excellent books on dog training available. (You can find the titles of some of them at the end of this book.) Here we'll just give you some highlights.

All the methods and tricks of dog training are variations on three main rules:

1. Praise the dog when it does something right.
2. Be firm when the dog does something wrong.
3. Be consistent.

Another important principle, which is sort of a subdivision of the third rule, is: Don't let your puppy get into the habit of doing things that seem cute now but will be a nuisance when it is a full-grown dog. Such habits include nibbling on your toes and ankles and jumping up. (Having a tiny puppy jump up joyfully to greet you may be charming, but it is less charming when it weighs fifty or a hundred pounds and is big enough to bowl you over. Our friend with the bulldogs says she is perpetually black and blue around the knees from the loving greetings of her pets. And the dog who came with our house—left here "temporarily" by the former owner while her new house was being built—was a huge German Shepherd that would dash up from a frolic in the pond to greet us when we came home, planting her sopping wet paws firmly on our shoulders.) It is very hard for a dog to unlearn bad habits.

Use simple one-word commands whenever possible, and be consistent in the words you use. Dogs are capable of learning a substantial amount of English (or French or Russian or Chinese, for that matter), but they are not very strong on synonyms. If you tell your dog, "Rover, come!" one time and then, "Get over here, you dumb dog!" the next, you will only confuse it. Here are some basic standard commands that other dog owners have found useful:

SIT!   (Sit down on your hindquarters.)

STAY!   (Don't move until I tell you it's okay.)

COME!   (Come to me—and right away, not when you feel like it.)

NO!   (Stop what you're doing this minute! It is making me angry.)

DOWN!   (Don't jump up.)

HEEL!   (Go over to my left side and walk along beside me like a good dog, instead of yanking me along on your leash.)

The tone of voice you use is very important. Praise the dog lavishly when it does something right, and use a happy, pleased tone when you do. Use a stern tone when you are scolding the dog for doing something wrong. And use a firm, no-nonsense tone when you are giving a command. A conversational tone is fine if you are sitting and having a conversation with your dog (which is perfectly natural, by the way; both you and your dog will enjoy it, and it may even seem to answer you), but when you are telling it to do something, you do not want to sound wishy-washy. Incidentally, a dog cannot really learn the difference between "right" and "wrong." But what it can learn is what makes its owner happy and what makes its owner angry; being firm and consistent will help to get that message across.

Hand signals can also be a help. When you are teaching a dog to "Sit" push its hindquarters down firmly with one hand. That is usually the easiest command for a dog to learn, and it can be very valuable later: if the dog is acting up and seems to have forgotten all its lessons, you can go back to "Sit" to get it back under control. When teaching "Come" and later when using it, make a beckoning motion with

A gentle push on the hindquarters can encourage a dog to learn the meaning of "sit!"

Courtesy Alvin and Virginia Silverstein.

your hand. A sharp downward hand motion helps to reinforce "Down."

Housebreaking can sometimes be a difficult and frustrating training problem. The secrets to solving it are to anticipate the dog's needs and praise it when it performs. If you live in an apartment, or if it is bitter winter weather when you get the dog, it will be best to start with paper training. One of the most effective methods is to spread newspapers all over the floor of the room where the puppy sleeps and be sure to get it back to that room at strategic times—right after meals and whenever it looks like it is straining. After a few days, when the puppy has the idea that it should urinate and defecate on newspapers, start picking up some of the papers. Praise the puppy when it eliminates on the papers and scold it when it does it on the bare floor. You need to *catch it in the act.* Neither praising nor scolding will have any effect if done afterward, because the puppy will not have the vaguest idea what it is being praised or scolded for. Rubbing its nose in its mess and spanking it will not only be useless, but it can also cause infections. As you continue to pick up papers, you will eventually be left with just one or two, and the puppy will have learned to eliminate only in that spot. (But don't be surprised if you are reading the Sunday paper sprawled out on the floor, carelessly leave it there, and then come back to find your dog has left you a present. It has learned that a newspaper is for only one thing, and that is not reading.)

To teach a dog to urinate and defecate outside, again you have to anticipate. Take it outside first thing after it wakes up in the morning, and again after each meal. Also try to grab it if you see it making straining movements or squatting, and whisk it out the door. As soon as it performs (*immediately*—dogs have short memories for that sort of thing) make a happy fuss over it. If you don't quite get to it in time and catch it in the act of eliminating on the rug, scold it severely. Soon it will be going to the door when it feels the need to eliminate and barking or scratching to let you know it wants to go out. Don't dawdle; if you do, the puppy will reward you with a puddle on the floor. You may find yourself wondering for a while exactly who is getting trained, you or the dog. But eventually, as the puppy gets older, it will learn to restrain its urges until a more appropriate time.

A natural form of puppy behavior may cause housebreaking problems. Puppies often urinate when they greet an older dog; probably the odor identifies the puppy as a young member of the pack, to be indulged and protected. Sometimes a puppy will greet its human owner in the same way and finds the human's disgusted reaction rather puzzling. Eventually it learns that this "submissive piddling" is not an appropriate greeting for humans.

If you live in the city, be considerate of your neighbors. Don't let your dog leave a mess right in the middle of the sidewalk or on somebody's front lawn. The proper place is in the street next to the curb. Many cities and towns have laws requiring dog owners to clean up after their pets, with a shovel and a bag or a special "pooper scooper." There are good reasons for such laws. Dog feces are not only extremely unpleasant to step into, but they can spread diseases. When you consider that dogs deposit 125 tons of feces and 100,000 gallons of urine on the streets of New York City *each day*, you can understand why dog wastes can be a major problem.

Did you know that a dog's barking can be a health hazard, too? Studies have shown that people continually exposed to loud noises develop high blood pressure and have a greater risk of heart disease. Continual barking can also make your dog less effective as a watchdog: if it barks all the time for no good reason, you will not bother to check when you hear it. A watchdog needs to be trained to bark when a stranger approaches, or when something unusual happens (like a fire in the house), but to keep quiet otherwise. If your dog tends to bark and howl whenever it is left alone, try leaving it and then return suddenly and scold it. If words don't do the trick, you may have to startle the dog by sharply slapping a folded newspaper against your hand, or even by jerking on its collar. (A choke collar should be used for training a dog. This is a chain that slips smoothly through a loop. It tightens around the dog's neck when you jerk on the chain, or when the dog pulls on it, but loosens again promptly when the pulling stops.) The dog may be barking because it is not getting enough exercise to work off its excess energy. This is often the problem with terriers, which tend to be barkers and yappers; an extra exercise run or play session may help to quiet the dog. If the dog barks at everyone who comes to the door, or continues to bark after a stranger has been properly introduced, try to soothe the dog, and if necessary, scold it.

Dog trainer Barbara Woodhouse suggests using a choke collar to break a dog of the habit of jumping up. Two people are needed: the owner or someone else whom the dog will greet joyfully and a second person to stand *behind* the dog and hold the chain. The owner returns, the dog jumps up, and the helper jerks sharply on the chain and commands, "Down!" The dog is startled (where did that command come from?), flops down, and the owner praises it lavishly. After a few practice sessions, the dog will think twice before it jumps up.

Most dog trainers recommend that a dog should never be hit with one's hand. If it is beaten regularly, it may become hand-shy. Then if you reach out to pat it, it may cringe away, thinking it is going to be hit. Or it may even bite in fear at a friendly outstretched hand. Instead, when scolding by voice isn't enough to make your point, swat the dog with a folded-up news-paper or clap your hands loudly to startle it.

Speaking of drastic measures to get a dog's attention, here's another word of caution: if two dogs are fighting, never get between them. If you do, you will probably be bitten. You can usually cool off a pair of angry dogs by dumping a bucket of water on their heads or, even better, by squirting them with a garden hose turned on full force.

FEEDING

After we got our dog Jacqui, the question of what to feed a puppy sparked some furious arguments in the family. Our youngest son was thirteen and a very conscientious soul. He read several pet manuals from cover to cover, avidly pored over the labels of cans, boxes, and bags, and consulted his dog-owning friends. As a result of all this research, he was convinced that a puppy should be fed only a specially formulated puppy chow and *nothing else*; otherwise it would refuse to eat its proper food and be *ruined forever*! Since one of us grew up with a rather nonchalant attitude toward dog feeding ("We always gave Rex table scraps") and the other was raised by a mother for whom wasting food was just slightly less sinful than murder ("Think of the poor starving Armenians"), our son's attitude led to continual conflicts. The question of cat food was a particular bone of contention. With four cats in the family, cats with typically variable and finicky appetites, there was often a bit of cat food left in their bowls. Since Jacqui adored every brand of cat food we used, it seemed thrifty to give her the leftovers, along with miscellaneous scraps from our table and shares of our snacks. (She loves grapes and apple cores.) Our son was horrified. "She won't get the proper *nourishment!*" he protested. The fact that the veterinarian commented on how healthy our dog looked when we brought her in for shots and noted that she was growing faster than the other puppies in the litter didn't seem to help.

Finally a friend whose daughter works in a veterinary hospital brought peace to our family. "Cat food?" she said. "Don't worry about that—dogs are crazy about it. Brandi says that when dogs at the hospital are too sick or listless to eat, they tempt them with a little cat food, and it perks them right up." As for table scraps: "There's nothing wrong with that. Dogs have been eating table scraps for thousands of years."

"But what about nutrition?" we asked. "And balanced diets? Kevin says Jacqui is refusing to eat her puppy chow because we spoiled her with people food, and it's going to stunt her growth."

"No problem," our friend said reassuringly. "Just give her a basic portion of the puppy chow, but mix in

147

some cat food or table scraps—whatever you have that day. That way she'll have her proper nutrition and some variety in her diet, too."

It worked. Kevin grudgingly accepted our friend's advice (and felt better about it when we found a dog manual, written by a veterinarian, that approved table scraps as long as they do not make up more than twenty-five percent of the dog's diet). Jacqui continued to eat and thrive.

We have read more widely since then and found

Dogs need a balanced diet just as people do, but an occasional snack —even of people food—will not harm their growth.
Courtesy Mary Bloom.

that some veterinarians advise using commercial dog foods (including special puppy chows for the first year, when the dog is growing actively), while others stress natural foods and give recipes for preparing your own mixes at home. What they do agree on is that dogs, like people, need a balanced diet, with adequate amounts of protein, carbohydrates, and fats, as well as vitamins and minerals. With their carnivorous ancestry, the dogs' protein requirement—especially meat proteins—is higher than ours, but cereal and vegetables are also good for them.

Here are some dog feeding tips. At each meal, offer your dog only about as much food as it will probably finish. This amount will change, depending on how actively the dog is growing, how much it weighs, and how much exercise it is getting. You can adjust the amount depending on how the dog acts: if it still seems hungry after it has cleaned out its bowl, give it a larger portion next time; if it leaves food uneaten, try offering a smaller portion. Don't leave uneaten food in the dish for the dog to nibble on between meals. The food may spoil, flies may crawl over it and lay eggs, and if it is outside, uneaten dog food may attract other animals such as stray dogs and cats, squirrels, raccoons, and skunks. If your dog refuses to eat anything at a particular meal, take its bowl away and don't offer it anything else until the next mealtime. Don't worry—the dog is not going to starve from missing a meal or two. Its ancestors lived a "feast or famine" life, gorging until their bellies were bulging when they made a kill and then going hungry until the next one. Among America's pet dogs today, over-feeding and overweight are the main problems, not starvation.

An occasional bone gives puppies good chewing exercise and some extra calcium. (Never use bones from poultry, which might splinter.) But too much gnawing on bones may wear down the tooth enamel of an adult dog.

Milk is a good supplement for puppies but is not really necessary for adult dogs. Whether you give milk or not, be sure that your dog has a source of water to drink within reach at all times!

It's best for your dog to have its own food and water bowls, and if you have more than one dog make sure that each one gets the same bowls at each meal. We have found that the heavy crockery dog bowls are more satisfactory than the plastic ones, which the dog may knock over or chew to pieces. But either way, keep the food and water bowls clean.

A word of caution: occasional food treats can be enjoyable for both dog and owner, and they can be useful rewards in training a dog. But avoid giving your dog a taste for chocolate. Large amounts of chocolate are poisonous to dogs; there have even been cases of dogs dying after gorging on a box of candy that an unwary owner left lying within reach.

HOW SMART IS YOUR DOG?

Anybody who has watched trained dogs perform in a circus or observed police dogs or guide dogs doing their daily jobs would say that dogs are very smart animals. Anyone who has sat and had a conversation with a dog and seen it listen attentively, pricking up its ears, barking or whining at appropriate points, and offering sympathy or cheerful distraction as needed, would say that dogs are very smart animals. Anybody who has watched our dog, Jacqui, wrap her chain around a pole and then stand there tugging futilely, unable to figure out that if she just walked around the opposite way the chain would unwind, would say that dogs are very stupid animals. (Or maybe smart after all, since she knows that if she does that we will have to come out and unwind her and give her some extra attention in the process.)

It is generally agreed that dogs are among the most intelligent animals, although they are not in the same league as monkeys. How do they stack up against cats? Dog lovers are convinced that dogs are more intelligent and point out how easily they learn to do tricks. (Actually, cats can be taught to do tricks, too, but they have to be in the mood to learn them and in the mood again later to perform them.) Cat lovers say that it depends on what kind of intelligence you are talking about. As people who have raised a number of each species, we were not at all surprised to read about the following experiment.

A psychologist named Adams trained some cats to pull lightweight but sturdy boxes by gripping a string attached to the box. Then he put a tempting piece of liver up on a high shelf. It was too high for a cat to reach by jumping, but he put one of the boxes with its usual string on the floor, not far away. A cat was let into the room and surveyed the problem, gazing at the liver. Then it went over to the box, climbed up on top of it, and tried to reach the liver. It made several attempts, but it was still too far away. Suddenly the cat jumped down off the box, seized the string, and pulled the box across the floor until it was under the shelf. It climbed back up onto the box, and this time it easily reached the liver.

The Adams test was tried on several dogs, but none of them managed to solve the problem of getting the meat. They didn't even try. They just stood there and barked.

This experiment illustrates the difference in the way cats' and dogs' minds work. Dogs are sociable animals, used to working in cooperation with humans and with other dogs. They tend to solve their problems by group actions, and if a situation seems beyond them their first impulse is to call for help. A cat, on the other hand, is a loner, used to working out solutions on its own. Is a cat smarter than a dog? Perhaps their intelligence is just different.

Courtesy Alvin and Virginia Silverstein.
Which animal is smarter?

Psychologist Kathy Coon has worked out an interesting dog intelligence test, using simple problems that any pet owner can set up. For example, one person holds the dog while another places a treat under one of three cups and then calls the dog. The holder releases the dog; it passes the test if it goes directly to the cup with the treat under it. In another test the dog must retrieve a treat that the tester has placed underneath an upside-down shoebox. (The dog passes this test if it gets the treat within fifteen seconds.) In other tests the dog must go directly to a ball that the tester has rolled under a chair, figure out how to get past a beach towel blocking the bottom of a doorway, and free itself from a sheet wrapped around it.

Kathy Coon tested a large number of dogs, both mixed-breed and representatives of all the main groups of purebred dogs. Standard poodles did the best, with an average score of 8.8 out of 10. Bulldogs and beagles did nearly as well (8.4 and 8.3). Among the breeds tested, Chihuahuas were the dunces, with an average score of only 2.2, Pomeranians averaged 2.8, and Siberian huskies scored 3.2. The average score for purebred dogs was 5.98, and mixed breeds averaged 5.80. Male dogs were slightly more intelligent than females (6.10 vs. 5.55). If you'd like to know how your dog compares, you can consult Kathy Coon's book, *The Dog Intelligence Test*, for complete instructions. (Our Jacqui passed eight out of the ten tests.)

SHOWING YOUR DOG

Many people who buy or breed purebred dogs look forward to the fun of competing in dog shows. The first recorded dog show took place in 1859, in Newcastle-on-Tyne in England. It featured sixty pointers and setters. Since then the idea has spread. In the United States eight thousand competitions are held under American Kennel Club rules each year, and most of them are dog shows. Judges examine the dogs and determine how closely each one measures up to the standards set for the breed. Some shows are limited to a particular breed or group of breeds; others are open to all breeds. In addition to these conformation shows, in which dogs are judged by their appearance, there are also obedience trials and field trials. In

In dog shows, dogs and their owners compete for honors.

obedience trials dogs and their owners or trainers perform a series of exercises designed to show how well they work together as a team. Field trials are special obedience trials that test the skills for which the dogs were originally bred. The AKC licenses field trials for scenting and trailing hounds, for pointing breeds, for retrievers, and for spaniels. (The hounds pursue cottontail rabbits or hares, the pointers point, the retrievers retrieve, and the spaniels flush out game birds and retrieve on command.)

In addition to the excitement of competition, winning "Best of Breed" in a dog show can make a dog extremely valuable as breeding stock and assure high prices for its offspring. (Neutered dogs and bitches are not permitted to compete in conformation shows, although they can take part in obedience trials and field trials.) A dog show can also be a social affair, a way to meet and greet people with similar interests. Often a whole family gets involved.

PUPPIES

With most pet animals the general rule is: if you want to have babies, you have to start with a male and a female. With dogs and cats, all you need is a female— as soon as she comes into season, the males in the neighborhood will find her.

Of course, if you want to have some control over what the offspring will look like, you will want to arrange a mating. This is especially true if you are the owner of a registered purebred bitch. Then you may wish to use a stud, a male who will father the litter. In the elite matings of the dog world, when sire and dam come from lines with long pedigrees, perhaps even

This Lhasa Apso pup is the result of careful breeding.

champion stock, generally the bitch is sent to the home of the stud during her period of heat. The mating is conducted under the supervision of the breeder who owns the stud. The breeder generally charges a fee for the dog's services—either money (perhaps $50 to $200) or the pick of the litter, or both.

Artificial insemination is another alternative: semen (fluid containing sperm cells) from the male is placed inside the female's body by a veterinarian. This approach spares the bitch a long trip to the stud's home and an upsetting stay in strange surroundings. Sometimes it is the only alternative: our friends with the bulldogs plan to use artificial insemination because bulldogs often have difficulty connecting on their own.

A bitch comes into her first heat at about six to eight months, but the experts recommend waiting until at least the second heat to breed her, after she has reached her full growth.

Just before her receptive period, the bitch will probably have a bloody discharge. This is perfectly normal and nothing to worry about; it usually lasts for about five days. If she is staining the rugs or furniture, you might want to use the sanitary napkins made especially for dogs to absorb the flow.

A few weeks after mating, the bitch begins to look a little round around the middle. Soon her appetite increases as the puppies are growing inside her. At this time she needs extra calcium and other minerals, and milk is good for her. After the fourth or fifth week her breasts begin to swell and get firmer. By the sixth or seventh week you can feel small lumps in her belly: these are the puppies. (Don't poke or squeeze them—you might damage them.) The bitch should be getting two meals a day at this time—with the growing puppies inside her body, her stomach does not have room to take in too much food at a time. She should continue to exercise regularly, but don't let her overdo it. By the fiftieth day her breasts may be swollen and full of milk, but normally the puppies will not be born until sixty-three days after mating.

About a week before the puppies are due, you can make some preparations. If the dog is very hairy, it is a good idea to clip the hair on her hindquarters and around her breasts. That will allow a more sanitary delivery and help the puppies to find the nipples more easily. Fit out a cozy nest box and encourage the bitch to visit it. A cardboard box will do, large enough for her to stretch and turn around inside. The sides should be low enough for the mother dog to get in and out easily but high enough to prevent the puppies from tumbling out accidentally. Line the bottom of the box with layers of newspaper or shavings that can be changed easily, and add some clean, soft rags. Don't feel insulted, though, if your dog ignores the nest box you have prepared so carefully and has her puppies in a closet or drawer instead. (One of us has childhood memories of a dog who had her puppies in the coal bin in the cellar.)

Some dogs prefer to be alone during the birth process (the technical name for it is whelping), but many appreciate the loving support of the family members. Unless complications are expected (in which case a veterinarian should be standing by), moral support is all you should give your dog. Just watch, give loving pats and soothing words, and let her take care of the details. One exception: if the bitch does not seem to be paying attention to a puppy after it is whelped and does not open and lick off the sac that covers it, you may have to help out. Very carefully tear open the sac near the puppy's head, then place it near the mother's head so that she will lick it clean. Her vigorous licking helps to stimulate the baby's breathing. (A pup can survive inside its sac for about eight minutes after birth.)

If the bitch appears to be straining for a long time without any results, if she shows signs of great distress, or if there are not as many afterbirths as there are puppies, call a veterinarian.

After the whelping is finished, the new mother will need to relieve herself. If you live in the city, it is best to keep her on a leash when you take her out: she may be a little groggy and not as careful as usual about watching out for cars. Offer her a light meal—something easy to digest, such as an egg yolk in a bowl of milk. Don't worry if she is not interested in eating: she may be too tired to bother, and anyway, she has received some nourishment from eating the puppies' afterbirths.

For at least the first few days, keep the mother dog and her puppies as quiet as possible. Family members should tiptoe when they come in to visit her, and *no one* should try to pick up the puppies. They are so tiny and delicate that they might be injured accidentally; besides, their mother has such a strong protective instinct that she may even snarl and snap at her owner. After a week or two you can start handling the puppies, very carefully and gently. Early contact with humans helps to socialize them and prepare them for

A doll's baby bottle or a similar-sized container should be used to feed newborn pups.

a lifetime of harmonious living with people. But don't disturb them while they are drinking their mother's milk.

If the mother dog does not feed her pups, you may have to hand-feed them. Dog's milk is much richer than human milk; a puppy grows much faster than a human baby and thus needs more nutrients. A satisfactory puppy formula can be made by adding cream to an infant formula for humans. The milk should be warm but not hot—about 100° F. You feed it to the pups with a doll's baby bottle or a medicine dropper. Usually young puppies need to be fed four to six times a day, which includes getting up in the middle of the night for a feeding or two.

Fortunately, most dogs know instinctively how to feed their babies, even if they have never had puppies before. Remember that the nursing bitch will continue to need extra food—up to three meals a day plus a snack at bedtime—and perhaps a vitamin and mineral supplement for her puppies, too.

Nursing comes instinctively to most dogs.

At about four weeks you can start giving the puppies soft solid food, such as the pureed meats for human babies. Soon they will be fully weaned and able to leave their mother. If possible, it is best to leave them with her until they are about eight weeks old.

CANINE BIRTH CONTROL

Watching puppies grow from birth on can be a wonderful experience, but trying to find homes for them when they are ready to leave their mother is not so enjoyable, and taking unwanted puppies to an animal shelter where they will probably be put to death is downright heartbreaking. Each hour about 1,500 unwanted cats and dogs in the United States are put to death, and each hour another 2,500 puppies and kittens are born. With statistics like those, one should think long and carefully before deciding to breed dogs.

The question then becomes: how do you *stop* your dog from adding to the pet population explosion? If you have a female dog you can try to keep her either locked in the house or under careful watch and safely away from all contact with males of her species during her periods of heat. But you will have to resign yourself to the fact that twice a year, for a period of several weeks, your dog may be restless, irritable, and constantly scheming to get out. In addition, she will be producing pheromones that float invisibly through the air and attract all the male dogs in the neighborhood. If you have a male dog, you can adopt a do-nothing course without suffering any direct consequences; but you will have a guilty conscience knowing that you are adding to a serious problem.

(And your dog will be more likely to wander and thus have more chance of getting into an accident.)

In 1978 the Food and Drug Administration approved an oral contraceptive for dogs—a canine version of "The Pill." It was to be available in a liquid form, and a pet food manufacturer even planned to add the birth control chemical to a special line of dog food. The pet food idea didn't work out, and few veterinarians prescribe the oral contraceptive today. Some vets are using injected drugs to stop a dog's cycles of heat from occurring, and an emergency hormone treatment is available as a "morning after" remedy when an unfortunate mating has occurred. But these treatments have very limited use, mainly by owners of purebred animals who wish to breed them at some time in the future.

For the average pet dog, the best solution at present is a surgical operation in which the reproductive organs are removed. The operation is called "spaying" for a female and "castration" for a male. "Altering" or "neutering" are other terms that can be used for either sex. The best time for the operation is at the age of about six months, before the first heat for a female and before a male has established a pattern of sexual behavior. Usually the dog stays overnight at the vet's and feels pretty much "out of it" when it comes home, but it recovers quickly. Neutering can make a dog less active, and it may tend to put on extra weight unless you watch its diet carefully. (Nobody seems to have told our Jacqui about that. We had trouble keeping her quiet for the recommended week after surgery, and as soon as her incision was healed she was a bounding bundle of energy again.) Spaying has the additional benefit of eliminating uterine problems and drastically cutting down on breast tumors. The main drawback to neutering is its cost: usually $35 and up for castration and $50 and up for spaying. But humane societies and some local communities sponsor low-cost clinics or free neutering for pet owners with financial problems.

HEALTH PROBLEMS

Fortunately some of the worst health problems of dogs are completely preventable. The standard "puppy shots" provide protection against distemper, infectious canine hepatitis, and leptospirosis. Some veterinarians also give injections against parainfluenza virus. Rabies shots are important for protecting both dogs and the people they come in contact with.

Distemper is a very contagious viral disease that produces fever, diarrhea, and respiratory problems (a runny nose and cough that may develop into pneumonia). Convulsions, mental confusion, and eventually death may follow. Young dogs are hit especially hard, but older dogs can suffer from it, too. If a puppy is breastfed by its mother, it will have protection from

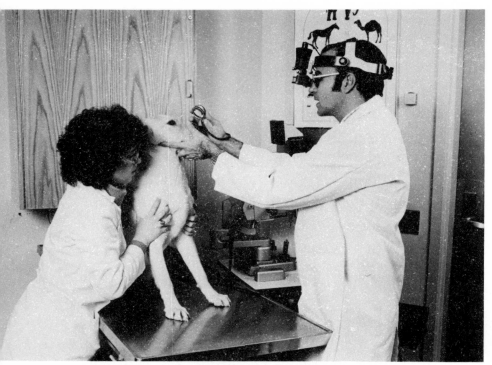

Courtesy School of Veterinary Medicine, University of Pennsylvania.
A good veterinarian can detect and treat most dog health problems.

distemper lasting for about six weeks, after which the series of shots will provide lasting protection.

Infectious hepatitis is a liver ailment that is fatal in twenty-five percent of the animals affected. Those who survive are weak and listless for a long time, and they can carry and spread the virus through their urine for months after they recover.

Leptospirosis is a kidney disease that can cause permanent kidney damage or even kill. Dogs can transmit it to humans through their urine. A three-in-one vaccine can protect dogs against distemper, infectious hepatitis, and leptospirosis.

Rabies is a viral disease that is nearly always fatal. It brings a horrible death, with agonizing pain. The virus is carried in the saliva and is usually transmitted by biting. Rabies has become much less common among dogs because of vigorous immunization campaigns, but there are still several hundred cases in dogs a year, and the virus is common among wild animals such as bats and raccoons. Dog licensing laws require proof that the dog has had up-to-date rabies injections, and most communities sponsor free rabies clinics each year. (A vaccine good for three years is also available.) The veterinarian who gives your dog its rabies injection will give you a metal tag. Fasten it to the dog's collar and make sure it is worn all the time. If your dog ever strays, the tag could help get it back to you. (It is a good idea to have an identification tag with your name and phone number on the collar as well.) If your dog happened to bite someone, the tag would be its proof that it is protected against rabies; otherwise, it might be killed.

A new viral epidemic among dogs that began to make headlines in 1980 is parvovirus. This disease was a mutation of a cat disease, feline distemper. (It is not related to the canine distemper virus.) Parvo is very contagious among dogs, although it is not transmitted from dogs to humans or between dogs and cats. It can be very serious, and in puppies it is often fatal; but only about half of the infected dogs show serious symptoms. As a result, an apparently healthy dog may actually be helping to spread the disease. Parvo is most common among dogs at dog shows and in boarding kennels. Fortunately, a vaccine against parvo was quickly developed after the disease appeared, and the cat vaccine for feline distemper also offers some protection.

Worms are a common health problem among dogs. A variety of worms can live as parasites in a dog's intestines. The dog picks up worm eggs in contaminated food and from the droppings of other dogs. Worms can even be passed to a puppy in its mother's milk. The veterinarian can test a sample of the dog's feces for worms, determine what kind it has, and treat it with various effective medicines. One type of worm, heartworm, is a serious health problem: the worms grow inside the dog's heart and can eventually kill it. Fortunately, heartworm can be prevented with daily pills prescribed by the vet.

An even more common parasite problem is fleas. These are tiny leaping insects that move about among the dog's hairs and suck its blood. The female flea lays her eggs in the grass or indoors in cracks on the floor by the baseboards. The eggs hatch into larvae that feed on bits of dust and dirt. They eventually turn into fleas, which hitch a ride on a passing dog. (If a dog doesn't happen to be passing, they can make do with a cat or a human.) Enormous numbers of fleas can infest a dog, leaving it scratching miserably. When it scratches, some of the fleas jump off and infest the house, the yard, and everywhere else the dog goes. If bitten enough times, most people become sensitized to flea bites, developing a sort of allergic reaction. Then each flea bite can develop into an angry sore that takes weeks to heal. Flea collars supposedly keep a dog or cat free of fleas for months; the ones we've tried have not been very successful. Flea sprays and flea baths can help to keep the problem in check. (There are also sprays to kill the fleas in the house, after you have vacuumed thoroughly.) But the fleas keep coming back. A product called Proban is taken internally and works by making the dog's blood toxic for the fleas. When the flea drinks, it is killed. But the drug is also somewhat toxic for dogs and must be given under strict supervision by a veterinarian. We must admit that the flea problem has us rather discouraged at the moment. Our vet tells us that last summer was the worst flea season he had ever seen, and this summer was even worse than that. We thought so, too. Recently researchers in Georgia reported that a commercial hand cleaner called Dirt Squad, made from the oil of orange peels, kills fire ants, flies—and fleas. The peel oil itself is even more effective. Orange peels are a throwaway product of the orange juice industry, so it should be possible to make a fairly inexpensive and effective killer for fleas and other insect pests. We hope so!

As for other health problems of dogs: if your dog acts listless or loses its appetite, if it develops a runny nose or a chronic cough or a sore that does not heal quickly and cleanly, if it continually scratches at its ears or patches of hair fall out, consult a veterinarian. If your dog is in an accident, the most important thing is to stop any bleeding. Use pressure bandages if possible, or if that doesn't work, a tourniquet. Keep the dog warm and quiet; if it seems to have broken bones, use the same sort of first-aid measures you would use for a human. You can moisten the dog's mouth, but it's best not to give it anything to eat or drink until you consult a veterinarian—and do that as quickly as possible. You should also get to a vet quickly if you suspect that your pet has eaten poison. One common poison that people often overlook is antifreeze. Both cats and dogs find antifreeze tasty and lap up spilled puddles of it. But it is a dangerous poison and can kill unless the poisoning is treated quickly.

Another avoidable danger to dogs is heat prostration. Never leave a dog alone in a car on a hot day. The sun beats down on the roof and heats up the interior of the car like an oven. Dogs—especially the short-nosed breeds like bulldogs and Pekingese—are extremely sensitive to heat. A dog can die in less than thirty minutes if it is left inside a car with its windows closed on a hot day. A few years ago a Kansas couple staying at a motel in Florida learned this lesson the hard way. Their motel did not allow pets in the room, and they left their cocker spaniel and poodle in their locked car for an hour and a half while they went to a meeting. They came back to find the car empty and a note on the windshield explaining that the dogs had been taken into protective custody by the local humane society. They could have been accused of cruelty to animals and would have faced sentences of up to a year in prison if they had been convicted. Instead, the president of the humane society suggested an alternative: the couple spent an hour inside their car in 92 ° heat under the hot sun, learning firsthand just what their dogs had suffered. The dogs spent the hour inside the society's air-conditioned building and greeted their owners happily when they got out.

Veterinarians have recently been seeing a trendy new dog ailment: jogging injuries. Dogs who run with their owners may suffer from sprains and strains as well as heat prostration. Running is good exercise for many dogs, and the shared activity of jogging is good for both dog and owner; but some dogs just aren't cut out to be athletes.

Even apparently healthy dogs can give health problems to humans. For example, dogs and cats may carry a microorganism called *Toxoplasma*, which passes out in their feces and can be transmitted to

171

humans. In most people, toxoplasmosis, the disease that this microbe causes, is rather mild—perhaps an intestinal upset or flulike symptoms. But if it occurs in a pregnant woman, it can be transmitted to her unborn child, resulting in blindness, brain damage, or even death.

Recently dogs have also been found to transmit the bacterium that causes strep throats. (The moral: don't kiss your dog and don't share a sandwich with it.) Puppies and kittens can carry cryptosporidiosis, a disease that produces diarrhea. Usually this disease is mild, but in people whose immune system is weak (such as those suffering from AIDS), it can be fatal. Researchers are also finding links between pet dogs and nerve diseases such as multiple sclerosis and amyotrophic lateral sclerosis (the disease that killed baseball star Lou Gehrig).

We hope we haven't depressed you with all this talk of health problems. Fortunately, except for fleas and worms, most dog ailments are not very common, and cases of transmission of diseases from dogs to humans are quite rare. If your dog is clean and well cared for, it should lead a healthy, contented life.

However, a dog's natural life span is much shorter than ours—less than ten years for some breeds and very rarely as much as twenty for any dog. This means that if you are a dog owner, you will probably have to face the death of your pet someday. Before the dog dies, there may be a few years of gradual decline as one body system after another begins to break down. There are drugs and various other treatments that can help make an aging dog more comfortable, but eventually you may have to acknowledge that your dog is suffering and is not going to get any better. Euthanasia, putting the dog to death painlessly, may seem to be the kindest solution. (The veterinarian can do it with an injection that takes effect within seconds.)

Psychologists are just beginning to recognize that a person whose pet has died may suffer grief just as deep and real as someone who has lost a human loved one. A number of clinics and private counselors are now offering counseling to help bereaved pet owners work through their grief and be able to live fully and love again.

Courtesy E. James Pitrone for The Seeing Eye.

174

Modern Dogs at Work

We live in an age of machines. In automated factories, huge machines weld automobile parts, pack cereal in boxes, and cut the cloth for dresses and suits. At home we depend on machines for household chores like washing and cooking; machines play games with us and answer the telephone when we are out; now there are even "pet" robots for sale, to keep us company. And yet, with all this growing dependence on machines, people are rediscovering the dog and learning all over again how useful our age-old helper can be.

Some of today's working dogs are doing the same kinds of tasks for which their ancestors were bred hundreds or even thousands of years ago. Hunting dogs have never really gone out of fashion, flushing out game or retrieving it for their owners. Watchdogs guard homes, farms, and factories. Bloodhounds track down lost children and escaped criminals.

Sheep ranchers are finding dogs the answer to a problem that has been costing them millions of dollars in lost lambs each year. Coyotes, wild relatives of the domestic dog, have a taste for sheep, and they are clever enough to take whatever they want from the ranchers' flocks. By the early 1980s, coyotes were killing more than a million lambs a year. The New England sheep industry had nearly disappeared: from the six million sheep that were raised in New England in 1800, the flocks had shrunk to only six thousand. Year after year, more farmers became discouraged as they saw half their new lambs killed by coyotes, and they gave up the sheep-raising business. Out in the West, ranchers are even more bitter about the coyote problem. At the Colorado Woolgrowers' Association convention in 1979, bumper stickers ironically suggested: "Eat more lamb. 10,000 coyotes can't be wrong."

Angry sheep raisers have tried many methods to get the coyote menace under control. They have trapped the predators, shot them from airplanes, and laid out poison baits. But the poisons often killed other animals, too, including endangered species like the bald eagle, as well as foxes, badgers, opossums, raccoons, and pet dogs. Now the use of poisoned baits is forbidden on publicly owned grazing lands, and shooting coyotes from airplanes is restricted. Sheep ranchers have tried other methods, such as outfitting their sheep with a poison-filled collar. (If a coyote tries to kill a sheep, it bites into the collar, gets a dose of poison, and dies.) Such methods are expensive and not very effective. Now the ranchers are turning to dogs as a safer, cheaper, and more humane way of coping with coyotes.

Not just any dogs will do. Herding dogs such as collies and German Shepherds are good at driving a flock from place to place and keeping the sheep from wandering off, but they need to work with human herders. What the sheep ranchers need are dogs that can live with the flock in distant pastures, guarding them faithfully even when the human masters are away for weeks at a time. Breeds of guarding dogs have been raised in Europe for centuries, and now they are being imported to the United States. One favorite breed is the Hungarian komondor, a big dog with a shaggy whitish coat that makes it look rather like a sheep itself. Other good sheep-guarding breeds are the Great Pyrenees from the mountains between France and Spain, the Maremma from Italy, the Anatolian and Yugoslavian shepherds, and the Kuvasz, a short-haired Hungarian relative of the komondor. These dogs, which cost $300 to $1,000 each, are being raised at breeding stations such as Hampshire College's New England Farm Center in Amherst, Massachusetts. The dogs are leased on a nonprofit basis to any sheep farmer who wants to try them, and the sheep raisers have been enthusiastic. Prospective sheep guarders are raised with flocks of sheep from

Courtesy Lorna Coppinger, Hampshire College, Amherst, Massachusetts.

These Shar Planinetz pups are being raised with sheep so that when they grow up they will feel like members of the flock and protect the sheep from predators.

puppyhood, growing up with the lambs and even suckling the ewes. As adults, they are gentle and placid, living peacefully with the sheep in their charge. The sheep accept and trust the dogs, and sometimes the dogs even help a ewe giving birth to her lamb. Farmers tell of komondors and Maremmas who licked the newborn lambs and cuddled them to keep them warm through the freezing nights. When danger threatens, the guard dogs fight furiously to defend their adopted family. Usually it does not come to a fight: a hundred-pound komondor, for example, is more than twice as large as a full-grown coyote, and the coyote is apt to just turn tail and run. Many coyotes won't even come near the flock if they catch the scent of dog.

There have been some failures in the new breeding program—dogs that have wandered off into the hills, or have been killed by traffic, or have turned out to be too lively and mischievous to get along with sheep; there have even been a few sheep killers. (One komondor at the New England Farm Center started an unauthorized breeding program of her own by running off with a herding dog. Her mixed-breed puppies wouldn't even let the farmer come near his flock, and then they ate some of the sheep they were supposed to be guarding.) But most of the dogs have been a great success. Hundreds have already been placed in more than two dozen states from New England to the Rockies, and sheep raisers are eagerly waiting for more.

Owners of Newfoundland dogs are teaching their pets to use an old skill for a new job. Newfoundlands are big dogs with strong bones, webbed paws, and thick double-layered coats. At home in the water, "Newfs" used to work for fishermen, swimming out to gather in the nets that their owners spread in the icy waters off the Newfoundland coast. These dogs also traveled on nineteenth-century sailing ships to help in emergency rescue work. Lloyd's of London, the famous insurance company, once awarded a medal to a Newfoundland who swam ashore with a line from a ship that was sinking off the coast of Nova Scotia and helped to haul the passengers and crew to safety. Another Newfoundland once saved the French emperor Napoleon from drowning.

Today Newfoundlands are used as lifeguards on beaches in France. In the United States, members of the Newfoundland Club of America are training their pets in lifesaving skills. Passing six junior tests earns a dog the title of Water Dog. Owners of a dog that passes the six senior tests can proudly call their pet a Water Rescue Dog. The tests start with a simple trial requiring the dog to go into the water and return to shore on command from its handler. Other tests range from retrieving objects from the bottom of a lake to towing lines and life preservers and hauling simulated drowning victims to shore. Not every Newfoundland can pass even the junior tests, but owners who take part in the training have fun and are proud to be teaching their pets such useful skills. As one New Jersey Newfoundland breeder remarked, "As long as people swim, there will be a job for Newfs. How many sheep need herding in New Jersey?"

An item in our local newspaper recently told about a new Armed Forces recruiting program. Uncle Sam wanted dogs, it said, and he was willing to pay up to $250 for each qualified recruit. There was no sex discrimination—either males or females could apply—and a dog did not have to be of any particular breed to enlist. There are some requirements though: the dogs had to be between one and three years old, stand at least twenty-one inches at the shoulder, and weigh at least fifty pounds. They had to be strong and agile, able to defend themselves, and not upset by gunfire. Special positions were available for dogs with a good nose.

The new recruits were to be trained for police dog work. Not only the military, but local police departments as well have found that members of the K-9 Corps (pronounced "canine") can provide invaluable help. A policeman's four-footed assistant can track down a suspect, help to identify him or her, and assist in making an arrest. Usually the dog relies on its nose for sleuthing work, but police in Everett, Washington, claim that their German Shepherd, Kento, used a different method. At a meeting at police headquarters, officers were shown a photo of a robbery suspect. As a joke, they showed the photo to Kento, too. Everyone laughed when the dog looked at the mug shot and sniffed. But later that day, while Kento and his handler were patrolling in a squad car, the dog suddenly began barking furiously at a group of people at a bus stop. Sure enough, the suspect was standing there.

Dogs with educated noses are sniffing out drugs and bombs for the police and military. In 1972 a German Shepherd named Brandy made national headlines and sparked a major federal project. A TWA jet had just taken off from Kennedy Airport in New York, bound for Los Angeles, when an anonymous phone call warned that there was a bomb on board. The airplane flew back to Kennedy, and as soon as it landed Brandy went to work. She sniffed out the bomb just twelve minutes before it was set to go off. Since then, dog teams have been installed in more than two dozen airports, so that any plane flying over the continental United States is no more than half an hour away from an airport with a "bomb dog" squad. These teams have already saved more than a hundred lives and prevented millions of dollars of property damage. The dogs are all male German Shepherds. They and their human handlers complete a twenty-week training program, and then they divide their time between regular patrol work and bomb squad assignments.

Dogs trained to recognize the smell of marijuana and other illegal drugs are patrolling airports, sniffing out drug smugglers. The U.S. Navy is using dogs to

Two military policemen from Fort Bragg, North Carolina, stand protected by their trained dogs. Fort Bragg dogs can be used for work on bomb squads, for sniffing out illegal drugs, and for security purposes.

control the problem of drug use by sailors. German Shepherds trained to sniff out marijuana are periodically taken through the living quarters at shore bases and aboard ships; the new nuclear aircraft carrier *Carl Vinson* was designed with kennels for seagoing canine detectives. On land, K-9 members of local police forces accompany their human handlers on raids of suspected drug dealers. Zekuno, a Rottweiler in southern New Jersey, ran up such an impressive record—more than one hundred arrests in two and a half years—that several attempts have been made to kill him, and he has now become a closely guarded "undercover" dog. The nose of a drug-sniffing dog is so sensitive that it often finds drugs that human investigators have missed. On one case, Zekuno kept barking and clawing at the back seat of a car, even though the police were unable to find any drugs. Finally the detectives ripped out the seat and found a single marijuana seed.

Nearly three hundred police dogs are working members of the famous Scotland Yard in England. In one recent year they aided in a total of 7,414 arrests, found 65 missing persons, and recovered 224 items of lost property.

Some of today's working dogs have more glamorous jobs, although they, too, must go through demanding training programs. These are the canine actors who star in movies, Broadway shows, and TV commercials. The shaggy mutts that have played Sandy in the stage and movie versions of *Annie* are just a few in a long roster of dog stars. The first canine movie star was featured in a seven-minute drama called *Rescued by Rover*. Made in 1905, the British movie told about a collie who rescued his master's baby from kidnappers. It starred Cecil Hepworth, his wife and baby, and his dog Blair. The movie was so popular that four successful sequels were made before "Rover" died in 1910.

One of the most famous canine movie stars was a German Shepherd named Rin Tin Tin. The story of his life sounds like a movie plot. He was born on a battlefield in France in 1918, at the end of World War I. American airmen rescued a litter of pups from an abandoned German dugout and named one of them Rin Tin Tin after a tiny doll that French soldiers carried for luck. When the war was over, Rinty went with his master to California, where he was trained for dog shows and then broke into the movies in 1923. In his nine-year career, Rin Tin Tin made more than forty movies, received ten thousand fan letters a week, and earned $1 million. In his films Rinty climbed walls (which had carefully camouflaged cleats to give him footholds), ran through flames (with his fur coated with fireproofing chemicals), and crashed through windows (that were really transparent panes of sugar).

Generations of children have loved the stories of Lassie, a faithful collie who found her way over a thousand-mile trek to return to her young master. The tale of Lassie first appeared as a short story, "Lassie Come Home," in 1938. It was expanded to a book in 1940 and became a hit movie in 1943. Film sequels and radio and television series carried Lassie's popularity on through four decades. Most people who have seen the Lassie movies or TV shows do not realize that the dogs that starred in them were actually males. A female collie was originally supposed to play the part, but she began losing her coat during the summer filming. Her understudy, a male named Pal, was quickly brought in to replace her. Since then, six generations of Pal's descendants (all males) have starred in Lassie films and TV shows.

Another sex switch occurred when the sequel to the film *Benji* was made. The original Benji was a mutt adopted from the Burbank, California, animal shelter in 1960. After a successful eight-year run as Higgins in the TV series *Petticoat Junction*, Benji was picked to star in the 1974 film about a dog who rescued two kidnapped children. When the sequel was filmed, the original Benji was already seventeen years old, too old to perform. His owner had been breeding Benji, hoping to produce a stand-in. Trying to match the appearance of a dog like Benji was quite an undertaking, since the shaggy little dog was apparently a mixture of

Courtesy Mary Bloom.
Not all working dogs lead a tough life.

cocker spaniel, poodle, and schnauzer. The descendant that looked and acted enough like the original Benji was a female. Benji II has starred in movie sequels, television specials, and made personal appearances all over the country, with no one suspecting that "he" is really a she.

Not many dogs can become movie stars. But thousands of highly trained dogs in the United States today are working in a very honorable profession: they are Seeing-Eye dogs, who guide the blind. The first Seeing-Eye dog was a German Shepherd named Buddy, who was born at a kennel in Switzerland. Buddy's owner, Dorothy Harrison Eustis, was training dogs of the German Shepherd breed for police and rescue work. In 1927 she wrote an article for the *Saturday Evening Post* about dogs being trained in Germany to help blinded war veterans. Morris Frank, a young blind man in Tennessee, heard about the article and wrote to Mrs. Eustis to ask if such a dog could help him. That letter led to a trip to Switzerland, where Frank spent five weeks caring for Buddy and learning to be guided by holding on to her harness. Buddy was with Morris Frank when he returned to the United States. Newspaper reporters were waiting for them at the dock in New York. They couldn't believe that a dog could safely guide a blind man through a modern city until Buddy led her master confidently across the street by the pier, through the heavy dockside traffic. Newspaper stories about the feat excited so much interest that Mrs. Eustis came to the United States to arrange for the training of guide dogs here. She founded The Seeing Eye, Inc., based

Courtesy E. James Pitrone for The Seeing Eye.

The final examination for each Seeing-Eye dog is a walk with a blind-folded instructor. Following behind (not pictured here) is the director of instruction and training who decides whether the dog is ready to be paired with a blind person.

189

in Morristown, New Jersey, in 1929. This nonprofit organization has been working since then to train guide dogs and win legal recognition for them.

Buddy spent the rest of her life touring the country with Morris Frank, demonstrating her skills for the benefit of Seeing Eye, Inc. They had many adventures: Buddy pulled her master out of the path of runaway horses, pulled him away from an open elevator shaft, woke him when she smelled the smoke of a fire in their hotel, and towed him safely to shore, clinging to her tail, when he grew tired during a swim.

Today's Seeing-Eye dogs are usually German Shepherds or golden retrievers. They must be at least fourteen months old before they start their special training. Guide dogs need even more self-control than the usual well-behaved pet. They must be obedient, and yet they must be able to *disobey* their owners' orders if the action would bring them into danger. They must be gentle and patient, and willing to curb their natural liveliness. A working guide dog is all business, with the job of leading its master or waiting quietly if he or she is busy. Guide dogs are trained to view people on the street or in buildings as obstacles to steer around, not objects of curiosity to sniff or bark at. After the Seeing-Eye dog has been trained in guiding skills, it is paired up with a blind person and the two of them spend several weeks together in supervised training, learning to work together.

Courtesy E. James Pitrone for The Seeing Eye.

Blind students spend twenty to twenty-seven days at The Seeing Eye learning how to work with their dogs. Each student is encouraged to groom his or her dog daily.

Restaurants, buses, and other public places may have regulations barring animals from entering, but these restrictions do not apply to guide dogs. Federal and state laws protect the rights of handicapped people to take their guide dogs into all places where the public is invited. The dogs' owners do their part by keeping their animals clean and well groomed, and the dogs are trained to be quiet and unobtrusive. A Seeing-Eye dog may lie patiently under the table in a restaurant for hours while its master eats and talks with friends. Often the other people in the restaurant do not even realize that the dog is there until its master gets up to leave.

Seeing-Eye dogs bring new freedom to the lives of the blind. Recently another nonprofit program has been training dogs to help the deaf. The Hearing Ear Dog Program trains dogs to alert their owners to important sounds, such as a smoke alarm, a ringing telephone, or a crying baby. The dogs are strays, adopted from animal shelters; most of them are mutts. First a prospective Hearing Ear dog recruit is put through a series of tests for intelligence, sensitivity to sound, and lack of aggressiveness. Then comes a five- to six-month training program in which the dog is taught to recognize key sounds and respond to them by running to a human and demanding attention with insistent pats of a paw or nudges with a cold nose. Then the dog leads the way to the source of the sound.

Several hundred Hearing Ear dogs are trained each year in five national programs. There is a long waiting list for the dogs, and many more could be used; the limiting factor is money. It costs about $3,000 to train a Hearing Ear dog, and applicants are charged only $150; the rest is made up by contributions from foundations, corporations, and private citizens. The dogs are carefully matched with their new owners. For ex-

Courtesy Red Acre Farm Hearing Dog Center, Stow, Massachusetts.
This Hearing Ear dog has just alerted and brought her mistress to her crying baby.

ample, an elderly woman confined to a wheelchair was given a Chihuahua because she would not be able to cope with a larger dog. Like the dogs that guide the blind, Hearing Ear dogs are permitted by law to accompany their owners everywhere. (They wear an orange collar and leash to identify them as trained hearing dogs.)

Guide dogs are not suitable for everyone. The handicapped person must like animals and must be willing to invest a great deal of time and effort in caring for the dog, grooming it, making sure it gets enough exercise, and working to build up its training and skills. Alyce Zee, a graduate student at the School of Social Work at the University of Pennsylvania, recently interviewed blind people with Seeing-Eye dogs in the Philadelphia–New York area. Ms. Zee, who herself is blind and depends on a German Shepherd named Heidi, asked the people she surveyed why they had obtained a guide dog and how they felt about their lives afterward. Most of the blind people said they got a dog to help them be independent or for protection; some said the main reason was companionship. About half to three-fourths had positive feelings about the changes the dogs had brought to their lives, saying that they felt more outgoing and had a better attitude toward their blindness.

When a partnership between a handicapped person and a dog does work well, it creates an intense emotional bond between them. Alyce Zee tells of an incident that occurred when she was riding on a train. Her dog, Heidi, was sleeping on the seat beside her, and someone criticized her for giving the dog a seat instead of having her sit in the aisle. "I said that dogs have rights, too," she relates. "She works hard, just like a human being, and she deserves a seat on the train." In some ways the dog seems closer to her than any human being could be. "Physically, socially, and psychologically," she says, "Heidi is an extension of myself. My well-being depends on her."

The special bond between a handicapped person and a guide dog remains strong even after the dog is no longer able to work. A few years ago a blind war veteran named Keith Roark made headlines with a search to find an ideal retirement home for his guide dog, Lottie. The German Shepherd's eyes were failing, but at the age of ten she could still have years more of life. Roark received more than eight hundred offers from families who wanted to adopt Lottie, and he visited more than ten cities to interview the most promising applicants. Finally he chose a young couple in San Antonio, who signed a contract promising to groom Lottie twice a day, take her to the veterinarian every three months, walk her at least a mile and a half each day, never leave her alone for more than an hour at a time, and feed her a special diet.

A guide dog owner in Nottingham, England, worked out an even more unusual solution to the problem of an aging guide dog who was going blind.

Sheila Hocken loved her faithful Labrador, Emma, so much that when she regained her eyesight in an operation she kept the dog and continued to care for her. When Emma lost her sight, her mistress declared, "She has been a tremendous friend, and now it's my turn to look after her."

One doesn't need to be blind to form a strong emotional bond with a dog, and some recent studies suggest that even the dogs who do nothing but live as pets are working dogs, too. They work as companions and therapists. The benefits they bring to their owners are very real. Tests have shown that patting an animal such as a dog or cat lowers the blood pressure. (Actually, it lowers the blood pressure both of the person who is doing the patting and of the animal that is being patted.) Since high blood pressure is a major risk factor for heart attacks, it might be expected that having a pet could provide some protection against heart problems. That is exactly what researchers have found. In one study conducted at the University of Pennsylvania, two groups of people who had survived a first heart attack were kept under observation. One group consisted of fifty-three people who either had a pet or were given one. The other group was made up of thirty-nine people who did not have pets. Within the first year, eleven of the petless people had second heart attacks and died. But in the larger group of pet owners, only three died of heart attacks during the same period of time.

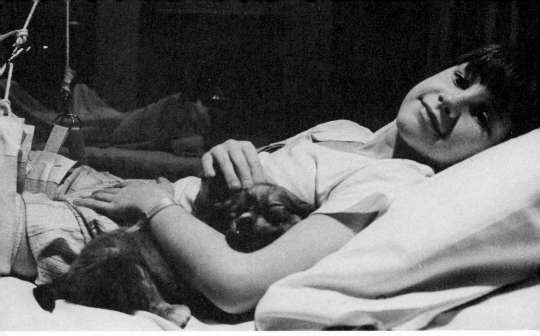

A visit from a pet can lift the spirits and improve the health of patients in hospital settings.

Hospitals and nursing homes have found that having resident pets or allowing animals from local shelters to come and visit can bring dramatic improvements in the health of the patients. The animals provide a new interest; the patients tend to talk about the pets instead of dwelling on the miseries of their own ailments. Often, disturbed children are calmed when they have pets to hold and care for, even when drugs and human therapists were unable to help them. Autistic children, unable to communicate with the people around them, have suddenly begun to laugh and talk after a visit from a pet. At the Lima State Institution in Ohio, pets are helping men classified as criminally insane. The men sent to Lima have committed violent crimes, and eighty-five percent of

Elderly people often cherish the companionship of a dog.

them have tried to kill themselves. But in the wards where the men are allowed to keep pets, there has not been a single suicide attempt in seven years.

For elderly people living alone, a dog can be a lifeline. Without the organized schedules of the working years, many old people tend to skip meals and fail to get enough exercise. But a dog needs to be fed and exercised in a regular routine and serves as a sort of time clock for its owner. The dog is also a friend and companion, someone to talk to and ease the loneliness. Perhaps the dog doesn't understand all the words, but it senses its owner's moods and responds to them with sympathy. A dog can also provide a sense of security, giving some protection against burglars and muggers and helping its owner to feel less fearful. Senior citizens with pets tend to have more regular habits and live more outgoing lives.

Unfortunately, many elderly people live in apartments or condominiums, and landlords may not permit them to keep pets. That situation may soon change, as more people recognize the benefits of pets to the handicapped and elderly. In 1983, Representative Mario Biaggi of New York and Senator William Proxmire of Wisconsin introduced a "pet amendment" to a housing bill, later approved by Congress. The new legislation prevents the owners of apartment projects who receive federal money from banning the ownership of pets by elderly and handicapped tenants. The landlords still have the right to create strict rules and standards, so that pets would not become a nuisance to other tenants or threaten their health and safety.

Courtesy Paul Duckworth.

The Dark Side

This is a chapter that dog lovers may be tempted to skip. We hope you won't. There are some facts about dogs that are unpleasant or sad, but they raise important problems that need to be faced and solved.

Each year more than thirteen million unwanted cats and dogs are destroyed in animal shelters. In addition, an uncounted number of family pets are abandoned to fend for themselves, living by their wits in the streets or woods. Some of them are kittens or puppies too young to survive on their own. Perhaps they will be found and taken in by kindhearted people ready to give them a new home; or perhaps they will die slowly of starvation or rapidly under the wheels of a passing car. Some of the abandoned animals are picked up as strays by dogcatchers and taken to animal shelters, where they might be lucky enough to be adopted into a new home but more likely will be killed. A fraction adapt to life on their own and become half-wild creatures, wary of humans, underfed, and plagued by parasites and disease. (Dogs on their own live an average of about two and a half years after they are abandoned.)

Why would anyone abandon a dog or a cat? Usually it is a tragedy of good intentions. The puppy in the pet shop or animal shelter or a neighbor's backyard looks so appealing; it seems to be begging, "Take me home!" Once home, though, the impulsive idea begins to lose its attraction as the adorable, affectionate puppy chews up everything in sight, has "accidents" in the middle of the floor, costs a fortune in dog food, and loudly demands constant attention. Eventually the puppy would calm down, but turning an unruly puppy into a well-mannered, obedient dog takes a great deal of time, effort, and patience. Not everyone is up to the challenge. When a person decides that getting a dog was a mistake, there is the problem of what to do with it. Finding homes for cute, appealing puppies is hard enough, but giving away a gangling half-grown dog or an adult dog that has picked up a few annoying habits is far harder. The local animal shelter is an alternative, but only a fraction of the animals taken to such a shelter are eventually adopted, and many are destroyed. "How can I condemn the poor thing to death?" the person thinks. "If I just drop him off a few miles down the road, maybe some kindhearted soul will take him in." And if no one does, at least the dog's former owner will never know about it. Abandoning an animal is a foolish and irresponsible action (in most states it is also illegal), but many people do it.

PUBLIC ENEMIES

Feral dogs—former pets that have reverted to a wild way of life—can be a nuisance or even a danger to people and livestock. They infect one another with diseases and parasites, and their droppings contain a variety of worm eggs and disease germs. Flies feed on the droppings and help to spread disease when they later alight on people or on uncovered food. Fortunately, rabies is rare. But since it does exist, a person bitten by a feral dog may face a nightmare. Often the dog runs away immediately and cannot be identified or recaptured. Without being able to observe the dog, there is no way of knowing if it had a legitimate reason for biting (perhaps defending its food or pups, or suffering from the misery of festering sores, or fearful because of past ill-treatment), or if it was really rabid. Unwilling to risk the possibility of dying in agony from rabies, the person will probably decide to have the painful series of antirabies injections.

About one million Americans (most of them children) are attacked by dogs each year, and the number is rising. Dog bites account for nearly one percent of visits to hospital emergency rooms. Half of the bites are minor cuts that need only a thorough cleaning and a swab of disinfectant. But ten percent of the bites require stitches and follow-up visits, and as many as five percent of dog bites become infected. (A dog's mouth may contain sixty-four different species of bacteria that can cause infections in humans.) Between one and two percent of the dog bites are so serious that the victim must be hospitalized, and about half a dozen people each year die from their injuries.

It is not only humans who suffer from the attacks of feral dogs. Last winter our local paper featured continuing coverage of a tense murder mystery. It started in December, when an unidentified animal began breaking into outbuildings in the nearby Bloomsbury area and killed about fifty rabbits and several chickens. The attacks occurred between midnight and six A.M. Footprints in the snow showed that the animal had large paws, about two and a half inches long. In each case it circled its prey first, then ripped open the rabbit hutches and chicken coops with its mouth, pulling out nailed boards and tearing through wire mesh with its teeth. The marauder killed the rabbits and chickens but left them uneaten and then went out to roll in the snow afterward. The state Bureau of Wildlife Services sent staff members over to investigate the killings and to advise the angry rabbit owners on how they might trap the culprit.

We followed the progress of the story with interest: the summer before, roaming dogs had visited our property in the middle of the night. In the morning, we found the roof and door ripped off our rabbit hutch, and patches of bloody fur were all that remained of more than a dozen rabbits. Our children were heartbroken. The young rabbits they had been raising were just weaned and were scheduled to be given to friends from school during the next few days. Our son, Glenn, pinpointed the time of the crime for us when he reported that he had seen several dogs on our property when he came home at three A.M. from a late-night session in the computer room at Rutgers University. They seemed quite friendly, he said; one of them came up to him wagging its tail. Another one seemed to be carrying something in its mouth, but it was too dark for him to be able to tell what it was. Later that morning the children received a small consolation when a young black and white Dutch rabbit hopped up to our door. We never found out for sure how it had escaped, but we were glad that it did.

The local paper continued to keep its readers informed on developments in the Bloomsbury murder case, and then, in March, a suspect was captured. She was a reddish brown hound dog, found inside a chicken coop. The suspect turned out to be innocent, though. She was gentle and friendly when she was captured, and a rabbit in a hutch next to the chicken coop was unharmed. The hound's paws were much too small to fit the telltale prints left by the Bloomsbury rabbit killer, and the people who had caught glimpses of a strange dog prowling in the area at the times of the killings reported that it was black and white, not reddish brown.

The story continued to unfold. SPCA officials thought they had discovered the owners of the hound dog and accused them of abandoning it. But the accused couple testified in court that the dog did not belong to them, and they were found innocent. Meanwhile, the hound gave birth to twelve puppies at the SPCA kennel, and eventually she and her children were all adopted. The rabbit killer was never positively identified, but neighbors reported on two dogs in the area that matched its description. The head of the county SPCA talked to their owners, and after that the killings stopped.

It seems that the Bloomsbury killer, like the dogs that killed our rabbits, was not a feral dog but someone's pet that had been allowed to run free. This is not unusual. Despite leash laws that require dog owners to keep their pets under supervision and confined to their own property, many people feel that such treatment would be too cruel for their dogs. Instead they allow them to run free and annoy the neighbors, terrorizing cats and joggers, leaving droppings on sidewalks and lawns, and disturbing the quiet of the night with their barking. Since dogs are sociable animals, pet dogs who run free often join with other free-running pets and with feral dogs to form packs. Then they may be not a nuisance but a

Dogfighting can lead to permanent physical injury and even death.

danger, capable of killing large farm animals and attacking humans. Just a few months before the Bloomsbury rabbit killer made local headlines, two German Shepherds believed to be someone's pets climbed over a four-foot door into a barn at a sheep farm in the area and slaughtered sixty sheep worth $150 each. The dogs were never identified, and the owner eventually sued the township for damages.

CRUELTY IN THE NAME OF SPORT

When we read of the cruel and brutal practices of

past centuries, we pride ourselves on how much more civilized we have become. Dogfights, for example, were once a popular sport. Bulldogs, mastiffs, and pit bull terriers were specially bred and trained to be vicious fighters, ready to struggle on to the death while eager spectators placed bets on the outcome. In England, where these dogs were originally bred, dogfighting was outlawed in 1835, and this sport is illegal throughout the United States as well. And yet, in some parts of the country (particularly in Louisiana, Missouri, Texas, and Maryland), dogfighting still goes on. Matches usually take place at dawn on a Sunday, in some out-of-the-way meadow far from town. Two-year-old dogs in top fighting condition go at each other ferociously in a circular ring six yards in diameter, while the owners and their friends cheer for their favorites and bet large sums of money. The owner of the winning dog winds up with a prize of perhaps $400 or $500, prestige among his friends, and a whopping veterinarian's bill to patch up his dog's battle wounds. Even the best fighting dogs rarely survive more than three fights.

Dog racing is a legal sport that can also be cruel in some ways. The greyhounds that race around the track chase a mechanical hare, but they are trained by releasing a live rabbit, which they are permitted to tear apart when they catch it. Greyhound racing is a fiercely competitive sport; more than fifty percent of the greyhounds born each year are destroyed by their trainers because they are injured or cannot run fast enough to qualify for the races.

Popular columnist Ann Landers has recently suggested that animal welfare groups should save their energies for fighting the "real atrocities" such as these, rather than compaigning so vigorously against the use of animals in scientific research.

A NOBLE SACRIFICE

It was a situation made for confrontation. In the fall of 1983 that perennial villain, the Defense Department, announced the establishment of a new Wound Laboratory. It proposed to buy dogs from animal shelters—unclaimed strays that were scheduled to be killed anyway—and use them to study the effects of gunshot wounds, trying to develop ways to save human lives on the battlefield. The dogs would be anesthetized before they were shot (with a 9mm Mauser from a distance of twelve or fifteen feet), and they would be painlessly put to death at the conclusion of the experiment.

The Defense Department scientists believed that the design of the experiments was humane—the dogs were doomed anyway and would not be suffering pain or distress—but animal lovers saw the matter differently. To them it was the latest and most blatant in

209

a series of offenses against nature and a prime example of human arrogance. In the flurry of public protests and denunciations, the Defense Department decided to delay the research program until the ethical aspects of the question had been studied further. Finally they decided to use pigs and goats instead of dogs.

Over the years, there have been numerous protests by animal welfare groups against the use of animals in experiments, particularly against the type of experiment called vivisection, in which surgery is performed on living animals. These protests have never achieved the complete ban on animal research that some of their backers would like, but they have resulted in the passage of laws setting strict standards for such experiments. Periodic surprise inspections of research laboratories, conducted under the Animal Welfare Act, ensure that the animals used in scientific studies are well fed and cared for and kept in clean surroundings with enough room to move around. (In fact, the conditions in research laboratories are much better than those in some pet shops, where overcrowding, poor diet, lack of opportunity for exercise, and filthy surroundings have been discovered.)

Sophisticated new tests that can be conducted on bacteria, fruit flies, or cell cultures have made it possible to cut back on the use of dogs and other animals in research and medical testing. Sometimes computers are used to simulate experiments without actually conducting them. For example, medical students at the University of Texas use a combination of two Apple computers to observe simulated physiology experiments. In one standard medical school experiment students would normally inject the drug epinephrine into a dog to observe the effects on its blood pressure, heart rate, and cardiac output. Instead, the University of Texas students press a key marked "E," and immediately the graphs on the computer screens show a jump in blood pressure and heart rate. In another experiment, students would cut open a dog's throat and pinch off the arteries. In the computer simulation, the student presses the "O" key and observes on the screen that the blood pressure rises and the heart output drops—and no dog needs to be killed. Yet with all these new animal-saving techniques, research in the United States still claims the lives of more than 60 million animals each year, including 161,000 dogs.

Experiments that seem both inhumane and unnecessary may actually be nothing of the kind. At the congressional hearings that resulted in the passage of the Animal Welfare Act, witnesses repeatedly referred to the Blalock press, "used in scores of experiments over many years to crush the leg of a dog." The implication was that this device was used frequently to torture defenseless animals, merely to satisfy the curiosity of sadistic scientists. Actually, however, the Blalock press was used mainly in an emergency research program during World War II. Doctors in Britain had discovered that people crushed under buildings that collapsed during bombing raids would be pulled out with seemingly minor bruises but then would die mysteriously within a week. Experiments on dogs revealed that protein seeped out of the bruised muscle tissues and eventually blocked the kidneys, causing them to fail. The Blalock press was used to reproduce this kind of injury. It was applied to the leg of a dog (which was anesthetized, so that it felt no pain) and bruised its muscles. (The device did not break any bones, as the antivivisectionists charged.) The dog experiments yielded lifesaving methods for preventing kidney blockage.

Indeed, dogs have played a key role in a number of important medical breakthroughs. The landmark experiments on the discovery of insulin were conducted on dogs. A young Canadian military surgeon, Frederick Banting, set up a private medical practice after the end of World War I and found that he had a lot of time on his hands. He spent the lonely hours between patients' visits reading medical journals, particularly articles on diabetes, which had just taken the life of a neighbor's child. Banting got an idea for a way to isolate the active hormone that normally keeps the body's storage and use of sugar well balanced. He took his idea to researchers at the University of Toronto, where he was assigned some laboratory space and a graduate student named Charles Best to work with him. The university support didn't include any money to run the experiment, but that didn't faze the two young researchers. They used stray dogs as their experimental animals, and Banting sold his car to finance the experiment. Working with the organ called the pancreas, Banting and Best isolated its hormone, insulin. They made dogs diabetic by removing the pancreas and then showed that injections of insulin brought the dogs back to normal. From the dog experiments, the researchers progressed to the treatment of diabetic humans. Today, millions of diabetics are able to lead normal lives through daily insulin injections; they owe their lives to the discoveries made in experiments on dogs.

Several decades later, laboratory beagles trained to smoke cigarettes provided the first firm experimental link between smoking and lung cancer. Before the animal studies, smokers and tobacco companies could argue that surveys of human smokers did not really prove that cigarette smoking could cause cancer and various other ailments. Our lives are so complex, they argued, that other factors might be to blame—air pollution, perhaps—rather than smoking. But in the experiments on dogs the conditions could be precisely controlled, so that only the effects of inhaled smoke were tested.

Dogs have also played a key role in the development of artificial heart valves, and surgeons practice the techniques of transplant surgery on dogs before trying them on human patients. Thousands of people are alive today thanks to a transplanted organ such as a kidney, heart, or liver. Thousands of heart attack victims have been saved by the prompt use of CPR (cardiopulmonary resuscitation) techniques. CPR is simple enough for the average person (even a child) to learn, yet effective in keeping vital blood flowing to the brain and other important organs until the heart attack victim can get medical attention. The basic techniques were developed by medical researchers using dogs.

Modern diabetes researchers are taking the classic Banting and Best experiments a step further by using space-age technology to develop miniature insulin pumps to deliver the hormone to diabetics more effectively. Traditional insulin injections deliver a big dose, which is gradually eliminated from the body. But the body's needs for insulin are constantly changing, depending on food eaten, exercise, and various other factors. At any particular time, the amount of insulin injected may not exactly match the body's needs. Programmable insulin pumps, small enough to be implanted in the body, can continually adjust the amounts of insulin being released into a diabetic's bloodstream, in much the same way the insulin levels are controlled by a normally functioning pancreas. In one current research program, such a programmable pump is being tested and refined in experiments on dogs in which diabetes has been produced medically.

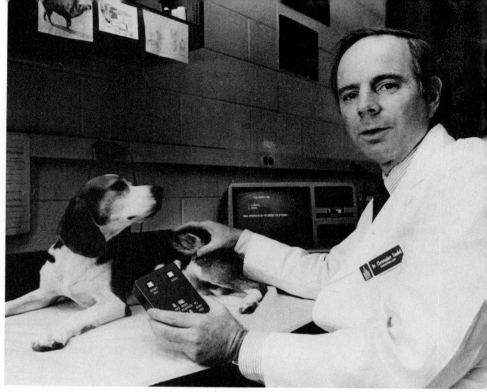

Research is progressing using an implantation insulin pump for the treatment of diabetes.

One group of diabetic dogs is treated with daily insulin injections, while another group has implanted insulin pumps. The dogs with the pump have fewer complications than those that receive traditional injections.

Unlike Banting and Best, today's medical researchers generally don't rely on strays for their laboratory animals: perhaps ten percent of the dogs come from pounds; the rest are purchased from breeders and often are specially bred for research. A strain of Brittany spaniels that inherit a disease very similar to ALS (amyotrophic lateral sclerosis, or "Lou Gehrig's

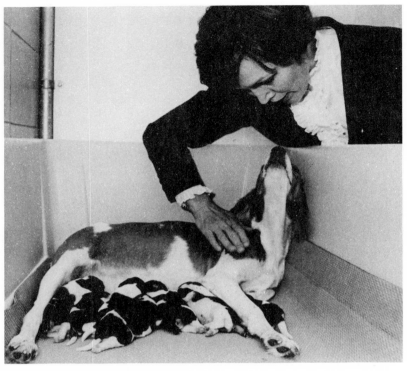

Courtesy David Harp for The Baltimore Sun.
Dr. Linda Cork at Johns Hopkins University is using dogs such as this litter of specially bred Brittany spaniel-beagle crosses to study a hereditary disease similar to ALS.

disease"), for example, is helping researchers to gain knowledge that may help human ALS patients.

Medicine is not the only field of science where dogs have made important contributions. The first animal to be launched into space was a dog named Laika. (Her name in Russian means "barker.") She was a passenger on Sputnik 2, which was launched in 1957. Radio transmissions from instruments attached to Laika's body informed the Russian scientists monitoring the flight that the dog had survived the launch and seemed none the worse for her experience. Unfortunately, space research had not yet progressed to the point of being able to bring a space capsule down safely, and Laika died when her Sputnik burned up on reentry. But in 1960 Sputnik 5 was launched and landed successfully, safely bringing back its crew of two dogs, six mice, and some insects. Studies of the effects of acceleration, weightlessness, and other conditions of space flight, conducted on animals like Laika, helped to prepare the way for the humans who later ventured out into space.

There is no doubt that experiments on dogs and other animals have helped humans, yielding drugs and techniques that have improved health and saved lives. Animal experiments can also help animals. Breakthroughs in veterinary science, such as vaccines that are saving the lives of millions of pet dogs and cats, would also have been impossible without animal experiments. And yet, do we have the right to use our fellow creatures in this way? Neal Miller, former president of the American Psychological Association, has this to say on the subject: "If, as the anti-vivisectionists claim, we don't have the right to exploit animals for research to relieve human suffering, we certainly have no right to exploit animals as pets, nor do we have the right to eat meat, eggs, drink milk, wear leather shoes or furs, sleep on down pillows, nor should we hunt or fish."

Wild Relatives

In an earlier chapter we compared the domestic cat to the domestic dog and commented that all cats are basically fairly similar, while dogs present an astonishing diversity. If we compare wild felids and wild canids, however, we find exactly the opposite. The wild cat species, from the diminutive Kaffir cat to the mighty lion, the fierce tiger, and the swift cheetah, are quite varied, whereas the wild dogs are surprisingly similar. (Most of them can even interbreed.)

THE DINGO

Many ages ago, scientists believe, the island continent of Australia was a part of the Asian mainland. At the time Australia broke off and the two land masses began to drift apart, nearly all the mammals in the world were marsupials, animals whose young complete their development inside a pouch on the mother's belly. When settlers came to Australia, they found an enormous diversity of pouched mammals. There were some that corresponded to kinds of animals found in the rest of the world, even though they were not related: pouched "mice," pouched "rabbits," pouched "cats," even a pouched "wolf," along with various unique species such as the teddy-bear-like koala and the huge, bounding kangaroo. But one native Australian mammal didn't seem to fit in. That was a wild dog called the dingo. It isn't a pouched mammal, it is very similar to the wild dogs of Asia, and it can interbreed freely with domestic dogs. Where did the dingo come from?

The mystery is solved when we realize that the dingo is not really a *wild* dog, but rather a *feral* dog— the descendant of domestic dogs that traveled from Asia thousands of years ago in the canoes of the aborigines who were the first human settlers of Australia. Fossils of dingolike dogs have been found in aborigine camp deposits dating back thirty thousand years. It is uncertain at what point the dingoes reverted to a wild way of life. Present-day aborigines sometimes capture dingo pups, tame them, and use them as hunting dogs, but they do not breed them. Like basenjis, dingoes do not bark but only howl or whine.

The ancient dingoes found Australia a hunter's paradise, teeming with game. Their only real compet-

THE DOG FAMILY TREE

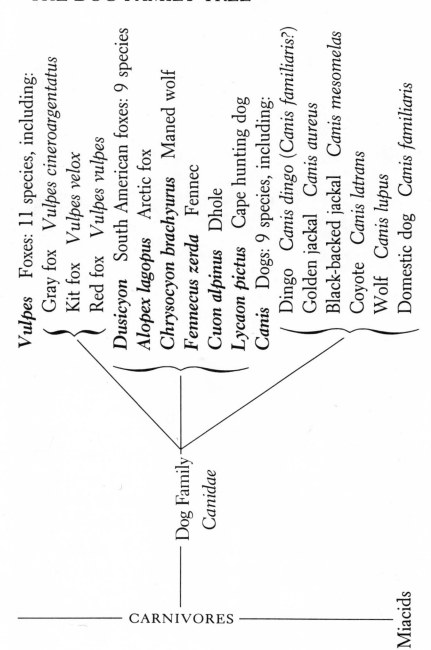

This female dingo is one of a colony bred at the University of Sydney in Australia. (Photo: N.W.G. Macintosh.)

itors were the marsupial "wolves." But these pouched mammals were not social animals; they hunted singly, running tirelessly after large prey such as kangaroos. The tawny-coated dingoes, which look like typical mongrel dogs, had inherited the cunning and social habits of their wolf ancestors. Hunting in small family groups, they were much more efficient than their marsupial competitors, who slowly became extinct. For a time the marsupial "wolves" survived in Tasmania, an island south of Australia, but many scientists believe that they have died out there as well.

When European settlers arrived in the eighteenth century, they imported sheep and cattle. Unfortunately, dingoes quickly developed a taste for this easy prey. A family of dingoes may kill twenty sheep or more in a single night's raid, far more than they can eat. Thousands of sheep and cattle are killed by dingoes each year. Like the ranchers in the American West with their coyote problems, Australian farmers have declared war against the dingo. They have fenced in grazing lands at huge cost, and they offer bounties for dingo scalps. At one time so many dingoes were being poisoned or shot that it was predicted they would soon become extinct. But nearly a century has passed since that prediction was made, and the dingoes are still plentiful, even in populated areas.

WILD DOGS

The wild hunting dogs of Asia and Africa are social animals with a close-knit community structure. They live in packs including several generations, and the whole pack works and shares together. Usually the males go out to hunt, running tirelessly after herds of antelope, wildebeests, and other grazing animals. In short sprints these dogs can run twice as fast as a healthy man, but they specialize in long-distance loping: they can run for as long as two days nonstop. Working together, the pack stampedes a herd and keeps it running until one or more of the weaker grazers tire and drop back. Then the dogs move in for the kill, seizing their prey in powerful jaws with teeth specialized for crushing bones. Quickly they gobble down as much as they can of their kill, then tear off pieces of meat to carry in their jaws. They bring the food back to the community den, where the females and pups, as well as the old dogs too weak for hunting, are waiting. The hunters unload their catch, putting down the meat they are carrying and then vomiting up the food stored temporarily in their bellies. Then the whole pack shares in the feast. Tiny pups and elderly dogs are allowed to feed right along with the victorious hunters; they don't have to wait for scraps as lion cubs do.

All the members of the pack are crazy about puppies. After the hunt, the adults stumble over one another, competing to feed and play with the pups. Females freely nurse other dogs' puppies and even try to steal pups from one another. If a female is killed, her pups (as many as a dozen in a litter) will be adopted by other adults in the pack. Both males and females have this strong nurturing instinct, and many litters of pups are raised by "uncles."

The wild hunting dogs are unique among the canids in having only four toes on each front foot, as well as on the hind ones. They do not bark, but howl with a yodeling cry that has been described as sounding like an oboe or the whinnying of a horse.

The Cape hunting dogs of Africa are often called "hyena dogs," because their coats are covered with

Courtesy Department of Library Services, American Museum of Natural History.
The spotted coats of these African hunting dogs are believed to serve as easy identifying labels for other members of the pack. (Photo: Martin Johnson.)

large dark spots in an irregular pattern. Some spotted animals have patterned fur as camouflage, making them hard to see, but this is not the case with the Cape hunting dogs, which stand out sharply against the open lands where they live and hunt. Scientists believe that the spotted patterns of their coats serve as identifying labels: each dog can recognize other members of the pack by sight over long distances according to the unique patterns of their spots. (These dogs have keen eyesight, which they use in hunting.) A hunting trip starts with a sort of canine pep rally.

225

During the heat of the day they stay in the den, napping or socializing. In the evening, one or two pack leaders go around waking up the others, nudging them or pulling on their ears. Soon all the dogs are awake, yapping, licking one another, and wagging their tails excitedly. Then off they trot, single file, to look for some game.

The dholes of India and Southeast Asia look very much like domestic dogs. A typical dhole is fox-red with a black-tipped tail, but pups in the same litter may vary from black to tawny yellow to nearly white. Because of this color variation, as well as their shape, dholes are often mistaken for domestic dogs. They are thought to be the ancestors of the dingo. Natives in Asia tell curious stories about the dhole's hunting techniques. They say that dholes urinate on bushes, then drive their prey through them, where they are blinded by the acid fumes of the urine. Another version is that dholes spray urine into the eyes of their prey by flipping it with their tails. Scientists are not sure whether there is any truth to these stories. (The second version would require some rather acrobatic running by the dholes.)

FOXES

The foxes are a rather varied group of small canids, including a number of species in more than half a dozen genera. (In the classification of animals, a genus [plural, genera] is a larger group than a species. The wolf, jackal, coyote, and dog all belong to the single genus *Canis*.)

To most people, "fox" calls to mind the red fox, sly Reynard of fables and fairy tales. This is the fox that hunters on horseback and their packs of dogs pursue in the elaborate sport of fox hunting. Found throughout Europe, Asia, and North America, the red fox is a handsome creature, with silky reddish fur, white on the chest, black "boots," and a long, bushy tail. Foxes usually take over burrows dug by woodchucks or badgers and then enlarge them, adding extra tunnels, a maternity room, and a number of escape entrances and exits. (One den in New York State, shared by two fox families, had a total of twenty-seven entrances and exits.) For part of the year the foxes live alone, but pairs of males and females (called "dogs" and "vixens") get together for the winter mating season. They work together to raise and teach the young (called "kits") and stay together until the young foxes go out on their own at the end of the summer. Usually foxes mate for life.

Farmers regard foxes as pests, and people tend to think of them as stealing chickens for a living. Actually, foxes feed mainly on rabbits, small rodents, frogs, birds and their eggs, and beetles. They are not exclusively carnivores: their teeth are modified for grinding vegetable matter, and they vary their diet with grass, ears of sweet corn, blueberries, cherries, rose hips, plums, apples, and grapes when they are in season. (The fable of the Fox and the Grapes may have had a grain of truth in it—but real foxes like sour grapes, too.) Foxes also act as scavengers, feeding on the carcasses of other animals' kills. When food is plentiful, foxes store part of it away in buried caches. They consider these hidden food stores their own private property and periodically make the rounds to visit them, even if they never eat any of the food. In the winter, when snow covers the ground, the food caches may save a fox from starvation—unless opossums, raccoons, dogs, or other foxes have gotten to them first.

A fox sneaks up on its prey and then pounces— much more like a cat than a dog. During much of the year it is a solitary hunter, but while the young are being raised foxes hunt in family groups. (Recent studies have shown that some red foxes do live in groups with a social structure and share in the care of the young.) In areas where farmers exterminate all the foxes, thinking that they have gotten rid of pesky vermin, they usually live to regret it. Without foxes to keep their numbers down, rodents multiply, devour grain crops, and spread disease. It's not too easy to wipe out all the foxes in an area, though. Like the foxes in fables, real foxes are rather clever creatures, which learn to avoid baited traps and develop techniques for outwitting hunting dogs. Foxes are surviving fairly well in general, and they can even live in towns, feeding on garbage. Unfortunately, they are major carriers of rabies and may infect dogs and livestock.

Red foxes use a curious hunting practice called "charming." The fox, spotting rabbits feeding, rolls on the ground to attract their attention and then begins chasing its tail like a playful kitten. The rabbits gaze, spellbound, while the fox seems to be paying no attention to them. Actually, it is gradually working its way nearer, until suddenly it straightens out and pounces on the nearest rabbit. Some naturalists think that this behavior may be accidental: the fox is merely being playful and then happens to notice its audience of potential dinners. But others point out that though the practice may start that way, a fox is intelligent enough to learn quickly that "charming" is an effective hunting technique.

The red fox prefers open areas, but the gray fox of North America lives in rocky regions and wooded areas where there is plenty of cover. Gray foxes climb trees like cats, clinging with their front paws. (Red foxes can climb trees too, but usually only when the trunks are slanted.) The gray foxes have a very short life span, rarely living more than eighteen months, but they make up for that in fertility: each female usually manages to produce one or two litters of more than four pups each.

The smallest of all the foxes is the fennec, a big-eared fox of Africa that is only twenty inches long from its nose to the tip of its tail. The fennec's enormous ears are like radiators that give off excess heat, helping to keep it cool in its desert home. The kit fox, which lives in desert regions of the American West, is another small fox with big ears and uses the same kind of "air-conditioning system."

The maned wolf of the South American pampas is actually a kind of fox. It is called the "stilt fox" because of its long legs. It goes bounding over the pampas after hares and other speedy prey.

The arctic fox has a coat that changes color, from dark silvery-blue in the summer to almost completely white in the winter. The color changes keep this hunter effectively camouflaged all year round. (This is not the "silver fox" of the fur trade, which is a color variant of the North American red fox.)

JACKALS

The jackal has a bad reputation that is largely undeserved. Its name is still used in common speech as a synonym for a toady: one who does the dirty work for someone else. In Shakespeare's time the jackal was described as "the lion's lackey"; it was believed that two or three jackals ran ahead of a lion like hounds, scented the prey, and barked or howled to inform the lion. The lion would make the kill, and after it had eaten its fill, its helpers would be rewarded with the leftovers. No one has actually observed this behavior, since jackals are nocturnal animals, sleeping in their dens by day and active mainly at night. The whole story was concocted from circumstantial evidence: people heard jackals howling at night, and then at daybreak they found jackals gnawing at the remains of large grazing animals.

Recently, however, naturalists have been going out into the field and actually living among the animals they study, observing them from carefully camouflaged hideaways at all hours of the day and night. Their studies have shown that although jackals are scavengers, feeding on the kills of other animals, they are also skillful hunters on their own. The main prey of these slender canids is gazelles, which they kill in typical dog fashion, running the prey until they tire and then slashing at them with their teeth. (One species, the black-backed jackal, typically goes for the gazelle's neck, while another, the golden jackal, typically goes for the belly.) Any food that cannot be eaten immediately is carried off and buried as a future supply. Jackals usually live and hunt singly or in pairs, although packs are sometimes seen. A jackal is a more effective hunter when it works with its mate: in one study in Africa, lone jackals killed their prey in only sixteen percent of their attacks, but jackals working in pairs were successful sixty-seven percent of the time. Golden jackals, which live in Africa, southeastern Europe, and Asia, also eat large quantities of insects, digging out beetles and termites, snapping up grasshoppers, and leaping to catch moths on the wing. They also feed on small rodents, hares, ground-nesting birds, and snakes. In their role as scavengers they will fearlessly drive off vultures from the remains of a kill or hang around the outskirts of a village yapping for handouts. The ancient Egyptian god Anubis, conductor of the souls of the dead, was pictured in the form of a jackal.

There is a strong bond among the members of a jackal family. When they are separated, they communicate by howling, and when they are back together again they greet each other joyfully, wagging their tails, nosing each other, and rolling over on their backs. The parents feed the young by regurgitating part of their own food, and they both lick and groom the pups frequently and thoroughly. During the mating season, courtship begins with mutual grooming.

The jackal pair defend a territory around their home den; both the male and female mark its boundaries with urine. Jackals have a curious manner of fighting, called body-slamming or hipping. The animal faces its rival, jumps into the air, and swings its body in a half circle to slam its hindquarters into its opponent. Body-slamming battles often occur when two jackals are quarreling over rights to a kill. Like other dogs, these canids rarely take their fights to the point of serious injury. They have a complex set of body signals to indicate dominance and submission; when one jackal backs down, cringing to show its submission, the other is a good sport about it, and they may wind up playing together.

COYOTES

Western ranchers have declared war against the coyote. Hundreds of thousands of these canids are killed each year, by guns, traps, and poison. Yet the coyote has not been exterminated; in fact, it is expanding its

The howl of the coyote, once a romantic symbol of the American West, is now a familiar sound to many Americans from coast to coast—even in the cities. (Photo: E.H. Baynes.)

range. The coyote used to be a creature of the American West, but now it has spread all the way across the United States to the New England states and up into Canada; coyotes can be found from Costa Rica in Central America to Point Barrow in Alaska, seven thousand miles away. When coyotes began to move into the exclusive suburbs of Los Angeles about twenty years ago, people welcomed them and enjoyed their romantic howling at night—until they were shocked and horrified by the death of a three-year-old girl, killed by a coyote on a street in Glendale.

The coyote looks like a small wolf; averaging twenty-five to thirty pounds, it is about as big as a medium-sized domestic dog and a third the size of a wolf. Its name comes from a Mexican word, *coyotl*, and it can be pronounced either in two syllables, with the final *e* silent (the way the cowboys of the Old West said it) or in three syllables with an "ee" sound at the end. In the New World the coyote fills the same place as the jackal in the Old World. It thrives in desert and semidesert regions where there is not enough prey for larger predators like wolves and feeds mainly on rodents, rabbits, and deer, along with insects, birds, fish, lizards, and various kinds of vegetable matter. (Coyotes love watermelons but take only the ripe ones.) If they had stuck to that diet, probably nobody would have minded their presence; but when humans settled the West, coyotes expanded their diet to include poultry, calves, and especially sheep. A coyote leaps on a sheep, fastens its jaws on the sheep's neck, and suffocates it.

Sheep ranchers detest coyotes and are incensed at government regulations limiting the weapons they can use to kill them. Yet naturalists who have studied these wild canids find them admirable animals. Coyotes mate for life, and the pair live together, defending their territory, cooperating in the hunt, and caring for their young. (In areas where game is plentiful, coyotes may band together in packs; but if things get rough they split up into pairs, which their relatives the wolves do not do.)

The coyote's scientific name means "barking dog." It is the only wild dog species that barks as freely and frequently as the domestic dog. The evening call of the coyote is part of the picturesque background of the West. Groups of two or three coyotes gather at dusk for a chorus. One starts with a series of barks that increase in volume, finally merging into a long yell. Other coyotes join in, and they bark for a minute or two. The sound dies away, and then, after a pause, it starts up again. Other coyotes answer in the distance, and their calls echo eerily in the night.

The Indians of the Northwest had a coyote god. He was a hero and a trickster, cowardly, crafty, deceitful, greedy, and ungrateful, and yet a mighty magician who brought order into the world. He taught men how to fish and hunt but then brought them death. The coyote is a fitting symbol for this kind of god: even its worst enemies concede that it is a clever creature. Coyote pairs have been observed using teamwork to catch their prey. For example, one hides while the other drives a rabbit toward its concealed position; then the first coyote jumps out and pounces, and the two share in the kill. The coyote's wariness of traps is legendary. One trapper tried again and again to kill a particular coyote, but each time the animal managed to spring the traps without getting caught. Finally the trapper buried an alarm clock near a trap. When the clock went off, the coyote was overcome by curiosity at the strange noise coming out of the ground; it went to investigate and walked right into the trap. Despite the coyote's shrewdness, ranchers are killing huge numbers; but the coyote continues to thrive. It has another weapon in its amazing adaptability. When hunters and trappers kill large numbers of coyotes in an area where food is plentiful, the remaining coyotes can quadruple their population in a single season. The average size of the litters increases from three to nine, and the number of females bearing young can triple from about thirty percent to more than ninety percent.

It seems unfair for the ranchers to try to exterminate all coyotes when only a small proportion are actually sheep killers. (Studies have shown that some coyotes will not touch a sheep even if they are penned with it and have nothing else to eat.) The problem is that it is very difficult to determine which coyotes are the sheep killers and even more difficult to predict which ones might become sheep killers. Researchers studying coyotes in Wyoming are coming up with some clues. They have found that coyotes raising young will kill much larger animals than they would normally eat on their own. They drag their kill back to the burrow for the pups to feed on. The researchers theorize that coyote pups raised by sheep-killing parents may learn this feeding technique and grow up to be sheep killers themselves. They took their experiments a step further by tracking sheep killers back to their dens and then killing all the pups in the den (but not the adult coyotes who had killed the sheep). Wildlife advocates were horrified, protesting that the researchers were killing coyotes who were not sheep killers (they weren't even old enough to hunt); ranchers were appalled at the idea of letting the adult sheep killers live. But in each case, lamb kills in the area dropped by an average of ninety-two percent in the week after the pups were killed. The adult coyotes, deprived of their pups, no longer had any reason to kill sheep. The researchers suggest that such coyotes could be caught and surgically sterilized so that they could not have any more litters. Then, if they defended their territory against other coyotes, they would keep sheep killers away from the area and ironically serve as protectors of the sheep.

WOLVES

People's attitudes toward the wolf, the ancestor of the domestic dog, have been a strange mixture of admiration, respect, and fear. The early humans, who lived the life of wandering hunters, actually coexisted with wolves fairly well. But when people began to domesticate grazing animals and adopted an agricultural and herding way of life, wolves became competitors. Like today's Western sheep ranchers who hate coyotes, the ancient herders began to hate and fear wolves. Legends and myths painted the wolf as a ferocious creature, lying in wait for unwary travelers and preying on herds and flocks. These beliefs were instilled from childhood with fables like *Little Red Riding Hood* and *The Boy Who Cried Wolf.* There were only a few myths to emphasize the positive side of wolves, such as the story of Romulus and Remus, twin babies supposedly raised by wolves, who grew up to found the city of Rome. Perhaps wolves were more fierce in the old days and really did kill unwary wanderers into their territory; but today's wolves are more likely to whimper and retreat if they encounter a human. (Wildlife biologists have captured many wolves in the wild simply by grabbing them by the scruff of the neck.) Of the few documented cases of wolf attacks on humans in recent times, most have turned out to be cases of rabid wolves, which were not acting normally. Meanwhile, humans have killed far

This exhibit at the American Museum of Natural History recreates the scene of timber wolves hunting in the snow in Arapahoe Park, Colorado.

more wolves than the other way around. Wolves have become extinct in Great Britain, and in many other regions they are endangered species. In Scandinavia, where Norsemen once named their heroes after wolves (Beowulf means "War Wolf") and pictured a wolf as companion to Odin, the chief of their gods, there are only about fifty wolves left.

In their home territory, wolves range over hunting routes that may cover more than a hundred miles, marked along the way by urine-sprayed scent posts. They live together in packs that are extended families, usually consisting of a mated male and female, several of their older offspring, and the juveniles, who are denied full membership in the pack until their second year. There is a rigid social order in the pack, which is led by a dominant, or "alpha," male. His mate, the "alpha" female, usually heads a separate social structure among the females. Elaborate rituals of dominance and submission are played out with body gestures and facial expressions. (Biologists have worked out a whole vocabulary of wolf facial expressions, including "licking intention," "antagonistic pucker," and "intimidating stare.") The younger wolves are continually testing the alpha male; when he becomes too old to lead effectively, one of the younger generation will win the dominant role.

The members of the pack work together in the hunt and can even bring down a thousand-pound bull moose. (They try to get him to flee and bring him down on the run, when he can't use his slashing hooves as effectively. If he stands his ground, they will look for easier prey, such as a moose calf or a sick, lame, or old animal.) At the kill, the alpha male and his mate start to feed first and then permit the other members of the pack to join in. An adult wolf may eat as much as thirty pounds of meat at a time; but then it may have to go without food for several days, until another kill is made. Back at the den, the wolves regurgitate part of the meat for the pups.

Wolves are playful and friendly with other members of the pack. After a meal they often have a sort of "community sing": one member of the pack points its nose in the air and howls. The others gather excitedly, wagging their tails, and join the chorus. Scientists are not quite sure why wolves howl. They speculate that it may be to round up the pack, or perhaps to advertise their territory to other wolves. Or perhaps they are just singing because they feel like it.

Occasional "lone wolves" are single animals that have been banished from the pack. They may be old individuals too feeble to hunt, or young ones who have challenged the pack's social order and lost. They trail along behind the pack, scavenging the leavings of their kills. Young lone wolves may do some hunting by themselves, and they may mate with other lone wolves to start off a new pack of their own.

In the dog's wild relatives we can see many resemblances, not only in the basic canid shape but also in the kinds of social behavior that permitted the long-ago almost-dogs to develop into our most faithful companion.

A Dog Sampler

The more I see of men, the better I like my dog.
                                        —Frederick the Great

The great pleasure of a dog is that you may make a fool of
yourself with him and not only will he not scold you, but he
will make a fool of himself too.   —Samuel Butler

To his dog, every man is Napoleon, hence the popularity of
dogs.   —Anon.

People often grudge others what they cannot enjoy themselves. [Moral of *The Dog in the Manger*]   —Aesop

A living dog is better than a dead lion.
                                        —The Bible: Ecclesiastes

Thou did'st call me dog before thou hadst a cause,
But, since I am a dog, beware my fangs.
          —William Shakespeare, *The Merchant of Venice*

If a dog's prayers were answered, bones would rain from the
sky.   —Turkish proverb

When a dog bites a man, that is not news, because it happens so often. But if a man bites a dog, that is news.

—John B. Bogart

The quick brown fox jumps over the lazy dog.

—Practice sentence used in typing

There is no doubt that every healthy, normal boy (if there is such a thing in these days of Child Study) should own a dog at some time in his life, preferably between the ages of 45 and 50.   —Robert Benchley

The biggest dog has been a pup.   —Joaquin Miller

Old Mother Hubbard
Went to her cupboard,
  To get her poor dog a bone,
But when she got there,
The cupboard was bare,
  And so the poor dog had none. —Mother Goose rhyme

"Is there any point to which you would wish to draw my attention?"
  "To the curious incident of the dog in the night-time."
  "The dog did nothing in the night-time."
  "That was the curious incident," remarked Sherlock Holmes.   —Arthur Conan Doyle

A un perro con dinero lo llaman "Señor Perro." [A dog with money is called "Mister Dog."]   —Spanish proverb

In the whole history of the world there is but one thing that money cannot buy—to wit, the wag of a dog's tail.

—Josh Billings

Who loves me will love my dog also.

—St. Bernard of Clairvaux

If you pick up a starving dog and make him prosperous, he will not bite you. This is the principal difference between a dog and a man.   —Mark Twain

Oh, the saddest of sights in a world of sin
Is a little lost pup with his tail tucked in.

—Arthur Guiterman

A dog teaches a boy fidelity, perseverance, and to turn around three times before lying down.

—Robert Benchley

No one appreciates the very special genius of your conversation as a dog does.   —Christopher Morley

The psychological and moral comfort of a presence at once humble and understanding—this is the greatest benefit that the dog has bestowed upon man.   —Percy Bysshe Shelley

Courtesy Mary Bloom.

For Further Reading

GENERAL

American Kennel Club. *The Complete Dog Book.* New York: Howell Book House, 1979.

Ashworth, Lou Sawyer, ed. *The Dell Encyclopedia of Dogs.* New York: Dell, 1974.

Boorer, Wendy. *The Love of Dogs.* London: Octopus Books, 1974.

Caras, Roger. *A Celebration of Dogs.* New York: Times Books, 1982.

Dolensek, Nancy, and Burn, Barbara. *Mutt.* New York: Clarkson N. Potter, 1978.

James, Douglas. *The Wonderful World of Dogs.* London: Octopus Books, 1976.

Marples, Richard, ed. *Encyclopedia of the Dog.* London: Octopus Books, 1981.

Mery, Fernand. *The Life, History and Magic of the Dog.* New York: Grosset & Dunlap, 1970.

Moscow, Henry. *Domestic Descendants* (*Wild, Wild World of Animals* series). Time-Life Films, 1979.

NATURAL HISTORY

Fiennes, Richard and Alice. *The Natural History of Dogs.* New York: Bonanza Books, 1968.

Lopez, Barry H. *Of Wolves and Men.* New York: Charles Scribner's Sons, 1978.

McLoughlin, John C. *The Canine Clan.* New York: Viking Press, 1983.

Tanner, Ogden. *Bears and Other Carnivores* (*Wild, Wild World of Animals* series). Time-Life Films, 1976.

Amberson, Rosanne. *Raising Your Dog*. New York: Crown, 1975.

Boorer, Wendy. *Dogs: Selection, Care, Training*. New York: Bantam Books, 1972.

Caras, Roger A. *The Roger Caras Pet Book*. New York: Holt, Rinehart & Winston, 1976.

Fox, Michael W. *Dr. Michael Fox's Massage Program for Cats and Dogs*. New York: New Market Press, 1981.

Johnson, Norman H. *The Complete Puppy & Dog Book*. New York: Atheneum, 1973.

Kinney, James R. *How to Raise a Dog in the City and in the Suburbs*. New York: Simon & Schuster, 1969.

Latimer, Heather. *Dogs: Everything You Need to Know to Care for Your Pet*. New York: Prestige Books, 1981.

Loeb, Paul. *Complete Book of Dog Training*. Englewood Cliffs, N.J.: Prentice-Hall, 1974.

Margolis, Matthew, and Swan, Catherine. *The Dog in Your Life*. New York: Random House, 1979.

McCoy, J. J. *The Complete Book of Dog Training and Care*. New York: Berkley, 1970.

Miller, Harry. *The Common Sense Book of Puppy and Dog Care*. New York: Bantam Books, 1963.

Riddle, Maxwell. *Your Family Dog*. Garden City, N.Y.: Doubleday, 1981.

Seranne, Ann. *All About Small Dogs in the Big City*. New York: Coward, McCann, Geoghegan, 1975.

Siegel, Mordecai, and Margolis, Matthew. *Good Dog, Bad Dog*. New York: Holt, Rinehart & Winston, 1973.

Tortora, Daniel. *Help! This Animal Is Driving Me Crazy*. Chicago: Playboy Press, 1977.

Vine, Louis L. *Your Dog: His Health and Happiness*. New York: Arco, 1971.

Woodhouse, Barbara. *Encyclopedia of Dogs and Puppies*. New York: Stein & Day, 1978.

————*No Bad Dogs: The Woodhouse Way*. New York: Summit Books, 1982.

JUST FOR FUN

Clarke, Timothy T., ed. *The Dog Lover's Reader*. New York: Hart, 1974.

Coon, Kathy. *The Dog Intelligence Test.* New York: Avon Books, 1977.

Maloney, William E. and Suares, J. C. *The Literary Dog.* New York: Berkley, 1978.

Warner, Rita. *Dogs & Puppies Coloring Album.* San Francisco: Troubador Press, 1977.

Choose a puppy that seems alert and active.

A young puppy needs frequent meals. (The newspaper on the floor will aid in housebreaking.)

Index

Italics indicate illustration.